Dream Come True

Book 1

Dreaming of Love Series

By: Vanessa Miller

Dream Come True

Vanessa Miller

Book 1
Dreaming of Love Series

Vanessa Miller
www.vanessamiller.com

Printed in the United States of America
© 2021 by Vanessa Miller
Reprint of: Heaven Sent

Praise Unlimited Enterprises
Charlotte, NC

Other Books by Vanessa Miller

Something Good (rel. March 2022)
Dream Come True
Once Upon A Dream
Forever
Family Business I
Family Business II
Family Business III
Family Business IV
Family Business V
Family Business VI
Our Love
For Your Love
Got To Be Love
Rain in the Promised Land
Sunshine And Rain
After the Rain
How Sweet The Sound
Heirs of Rebellion
Feels Like Heaven
The Best of All
Better for Us
Her Good Thing
Long Time Coming
A Promise of Forever Love
A Love for Tomorrow
Yesterday's Promise
Forgotten
Forgiven

Forsaken

Rain for Christmas (Novella)

Through the Storm

Rain Storm

Latter Rain

Abundant Rain

Former Rain

Anthologies (Editor)

Keeping the Faith

Have A Little Faith

This Far by Faith

Novella

Love Isn't Enough

A Mighty Love

The Blessed One (Blessed and Highly Favored series)

The Wild One (Blessed and Highly Favored Series)

The Preacher's Choice (Blessed and Highly Favored Series)

The Politician's Wife (Blessed and Highly Favored Series)

The Playboy's Redemption (Blessed and Highly Favored Series)

Tears Fall at Night (Praise Him Anyhow Series)

Joy Comes in the Morning (Praise Him Anyhow Series)

A Forever Kind of Love (Praise Him Anyhow Series)

Ramsey's Praise (Praise Him Anyhow Series)

Escape to Love (Praise Him Anyhow Series)

Praise For Christmas (Praise Him Anyhow Series)

His Love Walk (Praise Him Anyhow Series)

Could This Be Love (Praise Him Anyhow Series)

Song of Praise (Praise Him Anyhow Series)

~Prologue

Leah Davison's younger sister Tamara was moving to Atlanta to work for a local news station. By the line of cars in front of her parent's four thousand square feet, brick exterior home and the gospel music loudly playing, she could tell that the party had started without her.

Getting out of her car, she stood there for a moment, nervous about ringing the doorbell at the very same home she grew up in. Her parents bought the place when she was in fifth grade, and Leah loved everything about it. From the beautifully landscaped yard to the 5" hardwood floors, granite and stainless steel in the kitchen. The screened in back patio that was the perfect place to hang out on summer nights.

She hadn't been allowed in this home in over a month, but today she was here for Tamara, so she wasn't concerned if her presence made the rest of the family uncomfortable. Taking a deep breath, Leah rang the doorbell. She actually had to ring the doorbell in a house she grew up in. Leah still couldn't believe that her mother stripped her of the keys to the house. But she wasn't here to dwell on that today.

"I'm coming." Leah heard her mother say before the door swung open. Dang! She was hoping that her father would answer the door, but he was probably still taking it easy after suffering the heart attack that her family blamed her for.

"Hi Mom, I came for the party." Leah put her hands in the air and gyrated like she was ready to get in the house and dance to the music.

But the frown on Alma Davison's face caused her hands to flap back down.

Alma stretched her hand out like a stop sign. "Not today, Leah."

Leah rolled her eyes and jerked her head as if to say, here-we-go-again-with-this-mess. "Mom, you already fired me from my job, but you can't fire me from this family."

"I love you, Leah, but you have some growing up to do. And I need space and time before I can bring you back into the fold."

Leah pointed inside the house. "But everybody else is already here. Adam, Solomon, and Larissa get say their goodbyes to Tamara. I just want to spend time with my sister before she leaves for Atlanta."

But her mother shook her head. "You are not allowed in this house and you know why."

The door closed in Leah's face as tears sprang to her eyes. Yes, she could admit it, what she'd done to her family had been awful, but couldn't her mother just forgive already? Why did they have to treat her as if she was no longer a part of the family?

As Leah got back in her car and drove off, she declared, "I don't need them. They never wanted me to be a part of this family anyway. I'll succeed in life without the Davison clan." She popped her fingers. "Period."

~ Chapter One

Five months later... October - 2016

"Fashionable," "chic," and "stylish" were words normally associated with Leah Davison's sister, Tamara. But ever since Leah had signed on as an event planner with Events & Things she had upped her own game. Leah knew she would never be as beautiful as Tamara or her cousin Larissa. But if the attention she'd been receiving from men lately was any indication, she looked pretty good. To top it off, her boss had recently commended her on the wonderful job she was doing and hinted at a coming promotion.

Six months ago, Leah had been the public relations manager for her father's church. She had loved that job, and the loss of it—admittedly her own fault—had landed her in the awkward position in which she now found herself.

Her latest event was a party at a nightclub where the liquor was flowing freely, and Ned Turner—a former client who was too handsome for his own good, and for the good of unsuspecting women—had the audacity to strut into the club and crash the private party. Leah was tempted to ask security to show him the door, but she didn't want to draw attention to the uninvited guest—who, she was almost certain, had been stalking her. His presence could cost her that promotion, because her boss had already informed her about

8

the no-dating-the-clients policy. So, she just kept doing her job and prayed that he would go away.

Leah smiled as she handed her business card to a potential client. The guy was the CFO for one of the local banks, just like tonight's guest of honor, and he didn't look like the kind of man who spent his time worrying about how much things cost. Her favorite kind of client.

Then she noticed Ned inching his way toward her.

Leah excused herself, then ducked into the kitchen. She pressed her back against the wall and peeked out, making sure that Ned wasn't on her heels. Her pretext was checking on the meal preparations, so she stepped up to the chef. "How's everything going, Chef Darnel?"

"Everything is superb, Leah," he replied. "Now, what are you doing in here? You know I don't like lookie-loos in my kitchen."

Like most chefs she contracted with, Darnel was extremely temperamental. That trait always got on her last nerve. But his hors d'oeuvres never failed to impress her clients, many of whom requested specific recipes for various dishes he had prepared. So, Leah lived with his moods. "I was just checking to see if you needed help with anything."

"What do you mean? You don't have enough to do, that you need to scrounge for work in the kitchen?" He shooed her away. "Go see to your guests up front, and let me attend to my kitchen."

Leah wanted to object. After all, she was the one who had hired him, and figured that gave her the right to hide out in "his" kitchen. But Chef Darnel was not only known for his exquisite hors d'oeuvres; he had walked off numerous jobs screaming bloody murder for the smallest of infractions. And his contract allowed him to keep two-thirds of the contracted price, whether he acted like a

9

fool or not. Leah decided not to mess with him. "All right," she conceded. "I'll just go on back out there and check on my client."

With her head lowered, trying to avoid eye contact with Ned Turner, Leah returned to the party. All the while wondering how in the world she would manage to escape being noticed by her ex. If she didn't see him for the rest of the night, that would be fine with her.

All her pondering came to an end as she crashed right into him. "I—I'm so sorry," she stammered, looking up to find him staring down at her.

"No need to apologize," he said with a smile. "I was looking for you."

"You were? Uh, why?"

Leah could have kicked herself. Ned was one of the first clients she'd worked with at Events & Things. After she'd pulled off a successful event, Ned had called and asked her out. Leah had been flattered that such a handsome, accomplished man wanted to date her. He was the founder and president of a successful financial planning firm. She'd gone out with him a few times, only to discover that he had a serious personality defect. He didn't understand the word no, and had tried her one time too many.

"You haven't returned any of my calls in over a month," he said, "so I'm trying to figure out what's wrong with you."

In Ned's world, nothing was ever wrong with him; it was always someone else, hence the personality defect. She got a bad feeling when she was close to Ned. It was like God was sending her signals, telling her to run. Leah glanced around the room, hoping to catch the eye of one of the security guards, but the closest one was on the other side of the club.

Ned grabbed her arm. "Come sit with me. We need to talk."

She pulled free from his grasp. "There's nothing to talk about, Ned. I'm at work, and I would like for you to leave me alone."

Smirking at her with those cold, dark eyes, he said, "I'm not leaving until you talk to me."

Leah felt trapped. "Okay, Ned. If you want to talk, then we'll talk. But give me a minute. I need to check with my client to see if he needs anything." She walked back toward the front of the room, where the party was in full gear. Her client was celebrating like there was no tomorrow. And if the drinks and well-wishes that had been floating around the club were any indication, his friends weren't leaving this party anytime soon.

Tapping her client on the shoulder, Leah put on a happy face. "Things seem to be going well."

"Oh, Leah, there you are. My buddy Ned was looking for you a moment ago."

"I saw him," she said, then got right back to business. "I just wanted to see if you needed anything else."

He glanced around. "Nope. Everything's going smoothly. You weren't kidding when you said you knew how to throw a good party."

"It's my specialty." She looked over her shoulder at Ned, still standing awaiting her return. Then she glanced at her watch. "Look, if you don't need anything else, why don't I get out of here? I'll send in the cleanup crew in about an hour, and they'll clear everything out."

He nodded. "That'll work. Send the invoice to my office. Throw in some business cards, too. I have plenty of contacts I can hook you up with."

"Thanks. I really appreciate that." Leah backed away from her client, keeping an eye on Ned. She stood by the bar for a moment, pretending to be checking in with the bartender. The moment Ned took his eyes off her, Leah raced to the side door and ran out of the nightclub like it was about to be raided.

Unfortunately, she'd parked at the far end of the parking lot. By the time she made it to her car and grasped the door handle, Ned had caught up to her. "Get away from me!" she yelled at him, trying to open the door.

But he grabbed her by the shoulders and spun her around to face him. "All I wanted to do was talk to you, Leah."

"Leave me alone, Ned," she warned him. "I promise you, I will call the police if you don't stop bothering me."

"Oh, so now I'm bothering you? Funny, I wasn't bothering you when you were taking my money and eating for free."

"I didn't take your money. You paid my company, and I planned your event. But if I'd known then that you were a stalker, I never would have agreed to work with you." She'd never had these kinds of problems when she worked at the church.

"All you did was take my money," Ned snarled, his eyes taking on a crazed look. "You never wanted a relationship with me."

"Move out of my way, Ned." She reached into her purse as she backed up trying to create a bit a space.

"I'm not going anywhere. You are going to talk to me." He reached for her.

Leah pulled her mace out of her purse and sprayed him like he was a roach and she held a can of Raid. He buckled over, grabbing his eyes. She jumped in her car, locked the door before she sped off.

Never in all the years she worked at her father's church had she ever had to mace anyone. She missed her family, wished things were different. She wished that Bon Jovi song, *Who Says You Can't Go*

Home was written for her, because she desperately wanted to go home and be with her family.

~Chapter Two

Cory Parker woke in a cold sweat. He clapped his hands twice to turn on the lights. Where was it? He normally kept his cell phone on his nightstand. Throwing the covers off, he jumped out of his king size bed and stepped on his phone.

"Please tell me I didn't break it." Picking it up, and seeing no cracks, he wanted to breathe a sigh of relief but he couldn't. Not until he checked his text messages. It was four in the morning, but the job of an investment banker was never done. If he missed an important call, no matter the time of night or day, it could cost him, his career, his bonus and the promotion that was going to get him to the fifth floor at C & T Capitol.

Cory's promotion wouldn't come with the corner office reserved for the managing director. But he would get a nice office with a window. Not some manufactured cubicle style office where the walls didn't go all the way to the ceiling and the neighboring senior investment bankers could hear his conversations and possibly steal his deals.

No call or text had come through since he left the office at ten o'clock that night. He put his cell phone on the nightstand and rolled over to try to get a few more hours of sleep. The life of an investment banker was stressful. But he loved the hustle and bustle of the job. Loved that he was making over a million dollars a year, and loved that when this next IPO cleared he would receive ten to twenty million dollars as a bonus, depending on how well the Initial Public Offering goes. The time when a private company first offers shares of their company could either go well, everybody gets paid, or it could be a big dud.

Life was good, except for the stress... except for the fact that his family complained they hardly ever saw him anymore. And he'd missed so much church, the pastor had sent a search and rescue team to find him. Cory had assured them that he hadn't lost his love for God. Didn't he display that by faithfully paying his tithes each month?

After getting a couple hours of sleep, Cory stretched and yawned, then got out of bed. Rubbing the sleep from his eyes, Cory made his way to his home gym. He paid for a gym membership but didn't have time to go. So, one of the bedrooms in his three-bedroom penthouse apartment had been turned into an exercise room.

On his way to the gym, he passed by the den, which had been designed for relaxation. He didn't do much of that these days. An 18x24 size portrait of Erlene caught his attention this morning. She had been a beauty with that golden brown skin tone, high cheek bones, and one of those short cuts that Halle Berry used to wear.

Erlene had loved flowers and had planned to own a flower shop. She had so much potential. But lousy taste in men. Turning away from the portrait, he kept walking down the hall until he was where he needed to be.

Hopping on the Nordic Track treadmill, he turned on the television that was connected to the front of the treadmill. Cory hated running alone, but his personal trainer ran with him via the Nordic Track app on the screen. This guy ran down the beach, in

Paris or through mountains, whatever Cory was in the mood for that day. Today he chose the mountains of Tennessee.

He wished his personal trainer screen was hooked up to his rowing machine as well, but he finished his hike through the mountains of Tennessee, got off his treadmill, turned the 70-inch television that was mounted to his wall to CNBC.

Cory did ten minutes on the rower and then jumped in the shower. Once he got out of the shower, he perused his walk-in closet. He had a closet full of white, starched shirts. But every now and then, especially when he felt like he was in for an exciting day, he jazzed it up a bit.

He chose a multi-colored stripped geometric print shirt off the hanger and put it on. Cory then put on his Italian crafted black single breasted Saint Laurent suit. Glancing at himself in the mirror, he liked what he saw. His grandmother called him a redbone because he was light skinned. Not light enough to be mistaken for white, but too like for Grandma Roe's taste. She liked her men blacker than midnight and meaner than a rattle snake.

Grandma Roe had issues, but she'd been the one who made sure he went to college. Even sold her house to put up the extra money he needed. He would love her forever for that. He brushed his short cut wavy hair, picked up the scissors and did a snip-snip around his goatee.

Cory used his shoehorn to slide into his size eleven Italian leather black shoes. It was 8:30am, the limo was outside waiting and he was ready to take on the world. Due to the long hours he worked and the fact that he didn't arrive home until nine or ten most nights, the bank had a car on standby at all times for him. Cory was thankful for the limo because he'd had an accident after leaving work late one night about two years ago. That accident had left him with a reconstructed ankle and a limp. Compression socks and limo rides were the new normal for him.

His mother thought the hours he kept were crazy. But the junior investment bankers schedule were worse than his. They were usually at the bank until around two in the morning when they were working on a live deal. Cory had made his first million five years ago, just before he turned thirty-five. After that, he had been on a steady pace toward partnership. He would make ten million on this next IPO and partnership. Not bad for a skinny kid from the West side of Charlotte.

"Good morning, Sir." The limo driver opened the car door and handed him the Wallstreet Journal and a Grande, nondairy, iced shaken espresso.

"Good morning, Sam. You're always right on time with this." Cory thanked his driver for the iced coffee and newspaper then climbed in the back of limo. Sam had introduced Cory to iced coffee last year and he had to have it at least three to four times a week. He made sure Sam received a hefty tip each week which more than covered the cost of the newspaper and espresso.

"Is it going to be a good week for investing, Mr. Parker."

Cory lowered the newspaper and smiled. "It's always a good week for investing. You've got to be ready for the long game though."

They pulled up to his office. Sam got out of the car and opened Cory's door. "What time should I be here tonight, Sir?"

"I should be ready to go by ten." Cory got out of the car, newspaper and iced coffee in his hands.

"I'll arrive by nine tonight just case you want to do something wild and crazy and take off an hour early."

Handing Sam the Wallstreet Journal, Cory said, "I circled a couple of things you might find of interest. But don't hold me responsible if it doesn't pan out."

Sam tucked the paper under his arm and grinned. "The last tip you gave me paid my son's college tuition for a year. I'm not complaining."

Cory tsk-tsked with a finger motion like Dikembe Mutombo after he blocked a shot on the basketball court. "I'm not giving out tips, just observations." He didn't pass out stock tips to everyone he knew. But it made Cory feel good to help out a good brother like Sam Duncan. The man had five kids and a wife with a chronic illness at home. The struggle was real, and Cory was glad he had the brains and the finances to help out.

Cory put his headset over his ears as he strolled into the building. Music always pumped him up and got him ready to take on the world. Pharell Williams' *Because I'm Happy* was on his playlist right now. Cory bounced to the tune as he made his way to his office.

He noticed that not many of the junior associates seemed happy or excited about being there this morning. Heads down. Frowns on faces. What was up with them? There was normally an electric atmosphere in the air because money got juices flowing like nothing else, Cory knew.

Stepping into his office, Cory took off his headset. His eyebrow raised as he spotted R. L. McMaster, his boss, the managing director standing in next to his desk. The man couldn't sit for more than five minutes at a time. Cory wondered if he slept or if he was some kind of super-human that needed neither sleep nor rest. "Hey R.L. what brings you down here?"

R.L.'s office was on the fifth floor. The highest floor the Investment banking house had. Cory was on the third floor, trying to get where R.L. resided, but at least he had a cubicle office, and for now, Cory was content with his accomplishments.

"We've got a problem. And it's bad."

Cory stayed on top of his deals and his investments. Everything was running smoothly. It had to be. The live deal he was currently working on with Delish Foods was schedule for a live IPO at the end of next month. All of the investors were onboard and excited about making money. His client was happily planning his wedding to the love of his life and all was well. "I'm not aware of any problems. You know I stay on top of my deals."

R.L.'s lips tightened as he scrunched his button nose and ran a hand through his silvery-gray hair. "This just happened, and we've already had investors calling." He opened an Instagram video on his phone.

A blonde-haired, blue eyed… check that, dazzling blue eyed woman sat on her sofa holding a package in front of the camera. It was a snack pack of a pound cake sold by Delish Foods. This was a new item for Delish and it wasn't on the market yet. "How'd she get that pound cake?"

"We need to find that out, but just watch what happens next," R.L. told him.

What happened next was the woman opened the wrapper. "I don't eat a lot of sweets, but I've been craving some sweets, so I thought I'd try this new product a friend gave to me."

She took a bite of the pound cake, and then immediately threw up. Or at least is sounded like she was throwing up, they could only see the back of her head while she made gut wrenching awful sounds.

The woman's face appeared on camera again and she said, "This mess tastes like dog food. It's not sweet at all." She showed the package again. Then told them, "I wouldn't buy anything from Delish Food. Not unless they are selling actual dog food for my puppy."

R.L. put his phone back in his pocket. "It's gone viral. Over a million views already this morning. And the comments are terrible. Some saying they thought about trying this brand, but now they won't."

Cory took a gulp of his iced coffee. Sat the drink on his desk as his eyes darted to and fro. He couldn't think. Needed to think... of something. "This has to be a fake." He rubbed his head. He was going to need some aspirin. "We tasted all of Jeremiah's products before we took this deal on. The peach cobbler, the apple pie and the pound cake are all 100."

R.L. nodded. "I tasted them myself, so I don't disagree with you. But we don't need this kind of bad press. Our investors are getting nervous, so you have to do something or this whole deal will fall apart."

As R.L. left his office, Cory buzzed his assistant. "Sorry boss," Marcia Fields said as she rushed into the room.

Marcia was about five-two. Her hair was blue this week. Cory had seen it pink, brown and black as well. But that didn't bother him because Marcia was a work horse who got things done. "You knew about this?"

"I was helping Addison with one of our other investments when we saw the Instagram clip."

"Why didn't you call and give me a heads-up. I don't work like this and you know it."

She lifted a hand. "I swear I just saw it as you were walking in the building. By the time I got back to my desk, you were already in your office with the big guy."

"Get Jeremiah Thomas on the phone for me. Then tell the team to meet me in the conference room."

"Got it." Marcia headed out of his office.

"Oh, and Marcia. I need some aspirin."

She went to her desk and then came back with the bottle of pills. "I'll leave these here for you." She sat them on his desk and left, closing the door behind her.

Cory paced as he waited for Jeremiah to be buzzed into his office phone. If he couldn't solve this problem and fast, his ten-million-dollar commission was out the door. And he knew without R.L. telling him, that he could kiss that promotion goodbye. "Dog food? Who tastes pound cake and then says it tastes like dog food?"

His phone buzzed. Cory sat down behind his desk and picked it up. "Jeremiah, my man. How are you doing this morning?"

"Not too good. I'm guessing you've seen Lisa's performance on Instagram this morning."

Cory opened the bottle of aspirin. Plopped three tablets in his mouth and washed them down with is iced coffee. "You know the woman in that video?"

"I used to date her." Jeremiah didn't sound too proud about that declaration.

"Is she trying to get back at you for dumping her? Does she know about the scheduled IPO?"

"I don't even get why she's so angry. She cheated on me. I didn't even start seeing Kim until I broke it off with Lisa. The woman is out of her mind."

"How did she get the snack pack? Those aren't in the marketplace yet?"

"Kim had them at her house. Lisa must have taken one."

That didn't sit well with Cory. "Why would your fiancé be hanging around your ex and giving her products that haven't been released to the general public yet?"

Jeremiah took a deep breath then admitted, "They're sisters."

What! Cory wanted to scream into the phone. But he wasn't into judging his client. His job was to make them money. "We will need to send Lisa a cease-and-desist letter ASAP. And then we will most likely have to file a lawsuit against her to protect the IPO. Are you ready to do that? You're not going to be welcomed at the family picnics when we get through with your ex."

"Let me talk to Kim. I don't want her to be surprised about anything that has to be done."

"Jeremiah, I hope things go well for you and Kim, I really do. But my number one priority is to protect you and this IPO. You will need to be ready for the fight it's going to take to make this happen after the damage your ex has done."

"I hear you and I'm ready. Kim wants this as much as I do. She believes in Delish Food and is our top chef. So, she is disgusted by what Lisa did as well."

"Good. So, let me work with my team to see what we can do to stave off investor jitters. Some are already threatening to pull out."

He hung up the phone feeling as if he needed three more aspirin. He had dealt with enough vindictive women in his lifetime to know that they had a challenge on their hands.

~ Chapter Three

Bishop David Davison stood behind the pulpit looking regal. Like he was born to stand behind that pulpit and deliver the Word of God. Leah loved listening to her father minister. That is, until she discovered his secret child.

Everything was so much more complicated now. She entered the church through the back doors of the sanctuary, took a seat on the last pew and watched the service like an outsider. Leah wouldn't dare let her mother know that she was at church today, for fear that she'd be brought before the congregation and shamed as the daughter who caused all of their pain.

Her mother was seated on the front row. She looked as regal as ever with a stepping-in-to-spring yellow broad-rim hat perched on her head. Larissa was seated next to her and Solomon was scrunched up so close to Larissa, you'd think there wasn't enough room for him to scoot over on the pew. It was ridiculous that they let Larissa and Solomon carry on that way. But they were the favorite daughter and son now. Watching them caused Leah to think back to the last day she was with her family…

Leah Davison's father had been hospitalized, and it was all her fault. Now that he was back home and resting, she decided it was time to fess up. Leah came into the living room and sat down in a chair across from her parents. Her cousin, Larissa was seated in the chair opposite her. She put her hands over her stomach and leaned forward, biting her lip.

"Is something wrong, honey?" her father asked. "You look so sad."

"I have to tell you something, Daddy, and I'm just worried that you're going to hate me after I tell you what I've done."

He sat up. "I could never hate my own flesh and blood. Why would you even think a thing like that?"

Tears streamed down Leah's face as she said, "I did it. I paid Summer to accuse you of molesting her daughter." After she'd blurted out those words, her trickle of tears became a waterfall. "I'm so sorry. I'm so, so sorry for what I've done."

Other than Leah's crying, the room was silent for several beats before her mother took a deep breath, trying to calm herself. "Why would you do a foolish thing like that?"

Leah lowered her head. "As Daddy's public relations manager, I have full access to his files at church. One day, I found a file marked 'Solomon Harris.' I wasn't familiar with the name, and I was curious." She started crying again, then focused on her father. "You should have told us, Daddy. You and Mama had no right to keep the fact that you have another son from us."

"I'm sorry that I let you down, Leah," her father said.

The moment those words were out of his mouth, her mother stood up, outraged. "Why in the world are you apologizing to her?" She turned to Leah. "Do you know what you've done? Your father had a heart attack and almost died over that woman's allegations, and to discover that you had something to do with it...." Her voice caught. She started hyperventilating.

"Calm down, Alma," Leah's father said, his voice steady, gentle. "No sense in you having a heart attack and joining me on this sickbed."

"Please sit down, Aunt Alma," Larissa echoed. "Uncle David's right—you're getting way too worked up." She turned to Leah. "Can you just explain to everyone why you thought having this woman extort money from Uncle David was a good idea?"

Leah ignored Larissa and turned back to her mother. "I'm sorry, Mama." The look of outrage on her mother's face was destroying Leah.

"You're sorry. Is that all you have to say for yourself?" Exhaling, Her mother said, "Whew chile, I don't even know what to say to you."

"I was just so mad," Leah responded. As her mother started to get up again, she quickly added, "But I may have overreacted."

"Even if discovering that you had a brother upset you, I don't see the need for extortion." Larissa stared at her, completely confused. "I mean, Uncle David and Aunt Alma were not Christians and they were separated when Solomon was conceived."

"And that makes it, right?" Leah's eyes rolled heavenward.

"No, it didn't make it right, Leah," Alma lips were tight as she added, "But it was none of your business."

"This is a lot to take in right now. Can you help us understand what you were thinking?" Her father asked in a calm, even voice.

Leah pointed at Larissa. "Larissa and I are the same age. When it came time for me to go to college, you and Mama sat me down and told me that there wasn't enough money in the college fund for me to go to UCLA, my preferred college, and I accepted that because I knew that Adam was in college at that time, and that you would be footing the bill for Larissa's college expenses, as well."

"Your mother and I tried our best to save as much as we could for college, but we weren't earning as much in those days as we do now," her father tried to explain.

"Then how come Solomon was able to go to Harvard?" Leah demanded. *"Why wasn't he told to scale back on his college dreams and be a good little team player like I was?"*

"Your father had no say in Solomon's decision to go to Harvard, or any other school he might have chosen, for that matter," her mother said.

"I think you're allowing yourself to be deceived, Mama. Daddy practically has enough on Solomon to fill a scrapbook in that folder of his. And I'm willing to bet that you've never seen any of its contents."

Alma looked from her daughter to her husband. *"What is she talking about, David?"*

Sighing, Daddy turned to Larissa. *"Would you mind going to my office and getting that file on your way home from work tomorrow?"*

"Mama doesn't have to wait another day," Leah piped up. *"I can go get that file tonight and bring it back."*

"No, you've done enough," her mother said. *"I'll look at it tomorrow."* With that, she got up and started for the door. Before leaving the room, she turned back to Leah. *"I'd start looking for a new job if I were you. Because I'm going to begin looking for a new public relations manager for the church first thing tomorrow."*

Leah leaped out of her chair. *"You can't fire me. I work for Dad, not you."*

"Your father is in no position to run that church, thanks to you and that woman you hired to spew all types of false allegations at him." Alma huffed, then took a deep breath and said, *"Please clean out your desk. We'll give you two months' severance pay. That*

should give you enough time to find another job." With that, she left the room.

Leah didn't even know what she was doing sitting in this sanctuary. Her parents didn't want her around. It also didn't feel right being here without her sister, Tamara. But Tamara had moved to Atlanta for that television host job on a local channel a few months ago.

"Turn in your Bibles to the book of James chapter 4." Bishop Davison said. The congregation began flipping pages.

Leah averted her attention from the front pew back to the bishop.

"I'm going to be jumping around Chapter four and as I deliver my message you'll see why. He began reading…

"Forasmuch then as Christ hath suffered for us in the flesh, arm yourselves likewise with the same mind: for he that hath suffered in the flesh hath ceased from sin;

And above all things have fervent charity among yourselves: for charity shall cover the multitude of sins. Use hospitality one to another without grudging.

As every man hath received the gift, even so minister the same one to another, as good stewards of the manifold grace of God."

Bishop glanced up from his text, perused the congregation. "Don't go to sleep on me, because this is where it gets good."

Leah laughed and so did many in the sanctuary. Her dad used that same line often, and somehow it never got old.

He continued reading…

"Beloved, think it not strange concerning the fiery trial which is to try you, as though some strange thing happened unto you: But rejoice, inasmuch as ye are partakers of Christ's sufferings; that,

when His glory shall be revealed, ye may be glad also with exceeding joy. If ye be reproached for the name of Christ, happy are ye; for the spirit of glory and of God resteth upon you: on their part He is evil spoken of, but on your part He is glorified.

But let none of you suffer as a murderer, or as a thief, or as an evildoer, or as a busybody in other men's matters. Yet if any man suffer as a Christian, let him not be ashamed; but let him glorify God on this behalf."

Leah wondered if her father knew she was in the building. Was he trying to make her feel worse than she already felt? Yes, she had stolen papers from her father's office and tried to extort him for money because she had been angry about his secret child. She wished she hadn't done any of it. But now her father's message was telling her that she was an evildoer. A person not fit for the kingdom of God.

Larissa glanced in the back and then waved at her. Leah got out of her seat and slunk out the back door. The parking lot for the church was in the front of the building. As she walked to her car, Leah wished she could go back in that church and go to her mother... go to her father and beg him all over again to forgive her. But she was an evildoer, unworthy of forgiveness.

She unlocked her car door and was about to open it when Larissa swung the front door of the church open and ran over to her. "Don't leave, Leah. I have to talk to you."

Leah waved her off. "Not now, I have places to be. I was just dropping in for a quick minute."

"Wait, please wait." Larissa hugged her. "I've missed you. Why don't you come to the house for dinner today?"

Leah stepped out of the embrace. "My mother doesn't want me sitting at her dinner table."

"Leah, you're taking this too far. We love you."

Opening her car door, Leah flung back, "So, why hasn't my mother called me?"

"Why don't you come back in the church and ask her yourself?" As Leah sat down behind the wheel of her car. Larissa extended her hand. "I'm engaged, Leah. Solomon and I are getting married and I want you to be my maid of honor."

Leah's eyes bucked. Was-this-for-real? "You're always telling me how my father is like your father. So, isn't marrying Solomon like marrying your brother?"

Larissa's head bobbed back as if Leah had struck her. "Aunt Alma was my mother's sister, and Solomon is Uncle David's son, so you know very well that Solomon and I aren't related by blood. You're just trying to hurt me."

Leah scornfully said, "Why would I ever want to hurt you, Larissa? I mean, it's not like you've ever done anything to me, right?" She reached in her purse and pulled out a few of her business cards. "Look, I'm not sure if I can do the maid-of-honor thing, but if you need someone to plan the event you can call my office and I'll put you in touch with one of the event planners at the company."

"We're getting married in six weeks, so I'm not sure we have time to plan anything elaborate."

"Six weeks?" Leah gawked at her. "What, are you pregnant or something?"

A shadow of hurt passed through Larissa's eyes. "Solomon has moved his practice from Los Angeles to Charlotte. He bought us a house and we want to get married as soon as possible. So we can move in it together."

"Well isn't that just great for you and Solomon. While the rest of the Davison kids are miserable and wanting nothing to do with this family." She knew she was speaking for Tamara and Adam, her older brother and had no right to, but she didn't want it to come off as the only one miserable in this family.

"I love you, Leah. I want you to know that. And if you feel like I took some of the affection that Uncle David and Aunt Alma had for you, then I'm sorry. I never meant to hurt you. I only wanted us to be sisters."

Leah wanted to yell at her, remind her again how they weren't sisters. But Larissa was always so nice. It was as if Larissa was Cinderella and she was one of the evil step-sisters. Leah hated feeling like this, hated being an evildoer. She slammed her door shut, turned on the car and drove away before Larissa saw the tears that threatened to roll down her face.

Leah hadn't always been jealous of Larissa. They had once been best friends. She would beg her parents to allow Larissa to spend the night. Her cousin had been the best friend a girl could have. But then Larissa moved in and her mother doted on Larissa, forgetting she had two other daughters.

That wasn't entirely true. Tamara was the baby of the family, so she received extra attention. Not to mention that she was daddy's girl, through and through. And Adam had been sixteen, busy with sports and preparing to go off to college when Larissa moved in, so the attention didn't bother him. Leah had been the one left out. And she was still being left out.

The tears spilled. Once Larissa married Solomon, Leah would no longer be able to say she wasn't her sister, only her cousin. Leah hated that this made her sad, but the whole truth and nothing but the truth was that it did.

She picked up her cell phone and called Tamara. Her younger sister had left for Atlanta two months ago. When her sister answered the phone, Leah said, "Did you know that Larissa and Solomon are getting married?"

"Yes, of course I knew. She called me last night. I figured she'd tell you soon enough, so I didn't call you," Tamara responded, then asked, "Are you crying?"

"I've just got a lot on me right now and I'm not dealing with the idea of Larissa becoming my sister very well, I guess." She wiped some of the wetness from her face, but the tears kept coming.

Sighing into the phone, Tamara told her, "Are you really going through this middle sister drama again? You're thirty-five years old."

"I don't get what my age has to do with anything." Leah had called her baby sister for sympathy, but she wasn't getting it.

"Are you serious right now? Haven't you learned anything about this jealousy problem you have, from what you did to Daddy?"

This family would forever blame her for her father's heart attack. But it seems like everyone has conveniently forgotten what Daddy did. Leah scrunched her nose and scowled. "I'm not jealous. And she's not my sister. I was happy being her cousin and that's where she needs to stay."

"Larissa has been our sister since she was twelve years old and Mommy and Daddy adopted her. I guess I don't get why you could never accept that fact."

"Of course you don't get it." Leah rolled her eyes. Why had she even bothered calling Tamara? "You and Larissa are both so perfect, going after your dreams, while I sit here clinging to scraps."

"But I thought you liked your job?" Tamara asked, sounding confused.

"I did... I mean I do, I guess. It's just a lot going on in my life right now."

"You sound like you're on the verge of a nervous breakdown. Have you been praying? Remember how daddy told us not to come to him with a problem that we hadn't first taken to God?"

She pulled her car into her apartment building's parking garage and then turned off the ignition. She glanced in her rearview mirror and as she did Leah thought she saw Ned's blue BMW pass by. She convinced herself that she was being silly because a lot of people had that kind of car.

She focused her attention back on Tamara. "What if I'm the problem?"

"Then take yourself to God in prayer. I'm serious, Sis. Tell the Lord what's bothering you."

Leah wanted to take her sister's advice. She really did. But she didn't know if God was interested in anything she had to say.

She hung up with Tamara, then got out of her car. She took the elevator to the third floor where her apartment was. As she was about to put the key in the lock, her cell rang. It was Ned. She swiveled around to make sure he wasn't anywhere nearby. When she didn't see him, she quickly opened her door. Closed it behind her, and bolted the lock.

When the phone stopped ringing, she sat down on the sofa and blocked his number. She hoped he would get the message and leave her alone for good. She had told him numerous times that she no longer wanted to date him. Why couldn't he get that through his head.

If he kept bothering her, she would have to file a restraining order against him even though doing that would most likely get her fired. She wasn't supposed to date clients, let alone ensuring that they could never even enter the building where she worked.

~~~

Taking his robe off and hanging it in the closet in his office which was just ten steps away from the sanctuary, Bishop David said, "Don't you think it's about time to end this standoff between you and Leah?

Alma sat down on the black leather sofa. She had hand selected every piece of furniture and nick-nack in her husband's office. From the gray credenza with an antique mirror finish on the doors, where all of their family photos were displayed, to the handmade rustic décor sign hanging on his wall that said, 'when life becomes too hard to stand… kneel'. Everything in his office was put in its place to inspire her husband to do what God had called him to do. So, she wasn't about to allow a snake in the camp, no matter who that snake was.

Leah was their daughter and Alma loved her. But she had tried to bring her father's ministry to its knees and almost succeeded. As it stands, the once three-thousand member church had shrunk to twenty two hundred, with more leaving each week. "Trust me, David, your daughter has not learned her lesson yet. Let her sit in the wilderness for a little longer."

David sat down next to his wife, put his arm on the back of the sofa. "She's your daughter too, Alma. And she's hurting."

Alma gently touched her husband's jawline. It was stubbly because he hadn't had time to shave this morning. "I love how forgiving you are, and how much you love our children. But I cannot and will not allow anyone to tear this family or our ministry apart."

David stood. He went to the window in his office that faced the parking lot. Church members were headed to their cars or standing by their cars in conversation with others. "I call Leah to check on her from time to time," he confessed.

"Oh husband," Alma half grinned as she stood and walked over to the window. She took his hands in hers. "I've been married to you for over thirty years. You know me better than I know myself, and I know you the same way."

His eyes lit up as he smiled at her. "So, you knew I was staying in touch with Leah?"

Playfully punching his shoulder, she said, "Bishop David Davison, where your children are concerned, you are a big ol' softy. That's why I have to lay down the law on them."

~Chapter Four

Marcia popped her head in Cory's office. "The attorney is here to see you."

"Great, send him in." A few days had passed since the whole Delish Foods' pound-cake-taste-like-dog-food issue. Cory had met with his team and developed a plan he hoped would keep Delish Food's IPO headed for it's go-live date in five weeks.

So, with Jeremiah's blessings, the investment firm had hired an attorney. Cory stood and extended his hand as the attorney walked into his office. "Thank you for meeting with me on such short notice. I'm Cory Parker."

"And I'm Solomon Harris. I'm thankful that your firm thought of me. Especially since I'm new in the area."

Cory sat. "With the high-profile cases you've handled, we're lucky you set up an office in Charlotte."

Straightening his pants as he sat down, Solomon told him, "I have family here, so I decided that it was time for me to move closer and to get some church in my life. My father's a pastor."

"Oh really, what's the name of the church?" Cory asked, cocking his head.

"Christ Life Sanctuary."

Cory leaned forward. "You're kidding? I used to attend that church when I was a kid." Confusion settled on Cory's face. "I thought Adam was the only son Bishop Davison had."

"It's a long story." Solomon raked his fingers across his eyebrow. "I had a chance to view the Instagram video before it was taken down. She did a number on your client."

"Tell me about it." Cory shook his head. "The IPO had been rolling along, smooth as a baby's bottom and now, we just don't know."

"What we do know is that what Ms. Lisa Smith did was malicious and she intended to cause harm to his company, with full knowledge that Delish Foods was in the middle of the IPO process. And the fact that your client has other videos of this woman claiming to love his products," Solomon guaranteed him, "Let's just say, I can handle this case on my worst day."

"This woman is the type of scorned woman that goes after your money and the good name you work years to build. I went out with a someone like that years ago and it almost cost me everything," Cory said, thinking of Natasha Greenwald, the girl he had dated right after college. She had been his boss's daughter. When their relationship ended, she had accused him of rape. Fortunately for him, she had made false allegations twice before and her daddy had wised up to her games. Cory hadn't been arrested but he had lost his job and had to start over. No more vindictive women for him, uh-uh, no thanks.

That's tough, my man." Solomon shrugged. "But I know from experience that it pays to have the right woman in your corner."

Cory shook off the dust of his memory bank and kept it moving. "So you'll send Lisa a cease and desist letter and demand an open apology from her?"

"Yes, to both items. If she refuses to give the open apology, I will let her know that we plan to slap her with a massive lawsuit her grandchildren will still be paying off even after she's long gone from this earth."

A wry smile crossed Cory's lips. "I like the way you think, Solomon. So, while you're handling that, I need to find an event planner for Jeremiah's engagement party."

Solomon took a business card out of his wallet. "I can recommend an event planner. You might know her since you used to attend the Christ Life church."

Cory took the card from Solomon, glanced at the name. "Bishop's daughter. Leah was several years younger than me, but I remember her. She kind of tall for her age?"

"She's about five foot five."

"Wow, I thought she'd be a lot taller than that." He flicked the card against his hand. "And she knows her stuff? I need Jeremiah's engagement party to be an event that will restore confidence to our investors."

"My sister can do anything she sets her mind to. You have my word on it."

~~~

When they come for you, they come hard, was all Leah could think as she sat in the conference room listening to her co-worker talk about how successful her recent events had been. Donna Phillips had been in the event planning business for fifteen-five years, but that didn't mean she was better at getting the job done and understanding the special touches each event required.

Steven Johnson was a good manager. He just didn't understand when he was being played/ Like now.

Donna said, "Each of my events bring in at least two to three new events because I always solicit client referrals. I'm not sure our other event planners have learned that skill set effectively as yet."

One of Leah's co-workers said, "I'd love to be more effective at getting referrals. Maybe Donna could teach a class or allow us to tag along during an event or two."

Was this really happening? Donna didn't bring in anymore clients than anyone else. She just tooted her horn more than the other event planners.

"That's a great idea." Steven looked directly at Leah. "Would you be interested in learning this skill set as well?"

Oh, no he didn't. After all the business she had brought into this firm over the last three months, he wanted her to brush up on her referral skills? Before Leah could respond her phone rang. "Let me get this." She stood, lifted a finger, like she was walking out of the church sanctuary with that finger up, and walked toward the door.

"Hello, this is Leah Davison." She closed the conference room door behind her.

"Hi, you probably don't remember me, but we went to church together when we were kids."

Interrupting him, with a look of annoyance on her face, Leah said, "I'm sorry, I don't mean to be rude, but I'm at work right now."

"Exactly, that's why I called. Your brother gave me your business card and I would like to meet with you about an event I need help with."

It surprised Leah, that Adam was out passing out her business cards. But she would take the business anyway it came. "Who am I speaking with?"

"Oh, sorry about that. This is Cory Parker."

Leah's eyes expanded. "Are you serious… this is really Cory Parker?"

"It's me. I'm an investment banker at C & T Capitol now. I will need you to meet with me today if you want the job."

Leah took notes on the particulars, recognizing that this referral was going to be a big get for her. She told Cory she would meet him at his office within the hour. Then she went back into conference room, collected her laptop and purse.

"We're not done, Leah," Steven told her.

"Sorry boss, but I have to meet a new client. I can tell you more about it when I get back but I think it's going to be a pretty big deal." Leah had no doubt that if she reeled in business from a firm like Cory's, she would have that promotion. C & T Capitol was well respected in this town.

On her way out the door, she glanced back at Donna. "Don't think I'll be needing that class." She waved at her co-workers. "Bye now."

Twenty minutes later, she parked her 2001 Lexus 300 in front of C & T Capitol. She felt confident, wearing a lime green dress with gold pumps and pearls. A girl needed her pearls. Her oversized Fendi bag held her laptop, planner and a few pens.

Stepping into the office, her eyes took in the expansiveness of the place. The first floor held sofas and chair and a circular reception desk. There were five floors in this building. Leah could tell because of the open, circular floor plan that showcased each level with the ceiling being way, way up high.

"Can I help you," the receptionist asked while Leah stood staring up at the ceiling.

She turned to the woman. "Yes, I'm here to see Cory Parker."

"Is he expecting you?"

"Yes. He set up the appointment."

The receptionist handed Leah a clip board. "Sign in and can you please provide me with some identification."

Leah took out her driver's license and handed it to the woman. She then filled out the guest log.

The receptionist picked up the phone. "Mr. Parker, I have a Leah Davison here to see you." She hung up the phone and pointed toward the seating area. "You can take a seat over there; he'll be right down."

"Thank you." Leah sat on one of the chairs that lined the wall over by the elevators. She hadn't seen Cory since high school. Right before he left for college, her dad had all of the kids who were going to college stand behind him at the altar. Then her father gave all twelve of them a two-thousand dollar scholarship. All Leah remembered of Cory was how skinny he had been and that she and he were about the same height, even though he was several years older than her.

The elevator pinged. Leah shifted in her seat, and waited to see if Cory would step out. A short white man came stepped out of the elevator, followed by a young woman with blue hair. Leah thought she looked out of place in this grand building.

The young woman walked over to her and extended a hand. "Hello, I'm Marcia Fields. I'm Mr. Parker's assistant."

Leah stood and shook the girl's hand. "I'm Leah. But I guess you already knew that."

Marcia pointed toward the reception desk. "She told me where you were sitting. Follow me. I'll take you to Mr. Parker."

It sounded weird hearing Cory referred to as Mr. Parker. The skinny kid who she once threatened to beat up if he pulled Tamara's ponytail, was now a boss.

They got into the elevator and exited on the third floor. They walked past a cubicle area where she could hear different conversations about investments. If she had extra money after paying rent, food and her credit card expenses she would take notes.

When they arrived in front of an office that had Cory's name on the door, Marcia knocked and was granted entry. She opened the door. "Your two o'clock is here."

Before Marcia took a seat at her desk next to Cory's office, she stepped out of the way, so Leah could walk in.

Cory stood up and Leah tilted her head back to look upon his face. His gorgeous face. All she could think was, look what the Lord has done. "Well, it looks like you kept growing."

Cory's shoulders lifted a bit. He gave her the once over. "And it looks like you stopped growing, Ms. I'm-going-to-punch-you-if-you-don't-stop-teasing-my-sister."

Leah bust out laughing. It was a big, bold, I'm-enjoying-being-me and don't care who doesn't like it kind of laugh. "You remember that?" She balled her fist. "I would have punched you, you know."

"Oh, I don't doubt it." His eyes brightened as though he was basking in the memory. "Have a seat, before I do anything that would make you want to punch me again."

Back then, Leah had no doubt she would have knocked him over with the slightest punch. But brother-man has been working out. Cory had on a white dress shirt that showed off a well-formed and muscular upper body. She wouldn't be knocking *this* Cory over.

She sat down in front of his desk and tried to focus on the reason she was meeting with him today, but that stubbly beard looked so rugged and manly on his light skin, she was having trouble concentrating. Clearing her throat, just to give her mouth something else to do other than water over the delectable specimen in front of her, she said, "So, when did you run into Adam?"

Looking as if he was coming out of a trance himself, Cory squinted. "Adam?"

Why did he do that? Those thick eyebrows of his dipped dangerously close to his eye socket, making him look not just rugged, not just manly, not just deliciously gorgeous, but now he had a mysterious thing going on. "Is it hot in here?" Lean fanned herself with her hand.

"I was feeling a bit warm early, so I took off my jacket. I can ask Marcia to adjust the temperature if you'd like?"

"Please."

Cory picked up the phone and made the request. After hanging up, he turned back to Leah. "Now, what were you asking me about Adam?"

Leah wanted to pull out an envelope from her purse and continue fanning herself. She was sweating like a fifty-year-old woman in menopause. But the air kicked on in the room and she started to cool off. "I was just wondering when Adam gave you my business card."

"Oh. I guess I should have been a little clearer. Solomon Harris is working on a case for our firm. He's the one who gave me your business card."

Solomon strikes again. Leah didn't know if she had a problem with Solomon being her brother or the underhanded way in which her father handled the whole situation. He was looking out for her like a big brother should... and now he was marrying Larissa.

Maybe she needed to get over that too.

~ Chapter Five

In Cory's eyes, Leah had always been beautiful. When they were kids, he had tried to get her attention by picking on one of her other sisters. But then he had left it alone, because for one, Leah seemed to hate him and two, the four-year age gap when they were pre-teen and teens made a difference.

But the woman sitting in front of him now was certainly no teen. She had to be thirty-five even though see looked like she was in her twenties. Her eyes were hazel, but shadowy, like she was hiding secrets that would never be told. Her skin reminded him of coffee with a healthy dose of French Vanilla.

She had grown into her womanhood well, but it was nice to see that one thing hadn't changed. From way back since he could remember, Leah's hair had always appeared windblown. Her other sisters would have perfect cuts and hairdos, while Leah would look like a windstorm had gotten hold of her the moment she left the salon.

Today, her hair was in a bun, with disobedient strands flying all over the place. Cory loved her look. She was beautiful without even trying to be. But his IPO wouldn't get done if he kept staring at Leah rather than getting her onboard for the event he needed done. "I need to plan an engagement party."

"Give me a little information." Leah had notepad and pen in hand. "Is this your engagement party or someone else's?"

Leaning back in his seat, amusement danced on his face. "I wouldn't be making plans this late in the game if it were my engagement party. This is for a client. HE and his fiancé hadn't planned on doing an engagement party because he is launching his new company in about five weeks".

"I see. So, what made them change their minds?" She tapped the pen to the pad. "Will it be a big elaborate event or something small, for family only?"

"Your second question is easier to answer. So, I'll start there. Big and elaborate. We want newspaper coverage, magazine, the whole nine."

Leah squeezed her lips together. Her index finger waved the no-no-no sign. "Magazines require four to six months lead time."

"Delish Foods' initial Public Officering is in six weeks so don't have six months."

"Delish Foods?" She got excited. Scooted in her seat a bit. "Isn't that the company who makes those scrumptious peach cobblers?"

"What about on-line magazines? We need to create buzz, feel good stories around the happy couple and the desserts they fell in lover over... or something sappy like that."

"We can create buzz, that's not a problem.

Rubbing his hands together, Cory was starting to feel good about this project. "One and the same. However, let me explain our issue so you can be clear on the event and the publicity we need to generate from the event."

Leah asked, "Do you have a publicist in mind, or should I hire one for this event?"

"My schedule is too hectic, so if you became the event planner, you would have to take care of the publicity or be able to hire someone who can."

She nodded. "That works. My firm has relationships with a few publicists. I can make this happen for you. But it will be an up charge item in the bid if you're okay with that?"

He waved that off. "My client will become a billionaire once his company goes public. He won't mind spending to get this done."

As Leah began jotting a few things down, Cory told her. "A week ago, my client's ex-girlfriend went live on Instagram and pretended to vomit while eating a pound cake from Delish Foods, claiming it tasted like dog food. Her antics has made our investors nervous."

Leah's eyes widened. "The desserts I've tasted from Delish are everything. So, she has to be lying."

"I know, right." Cory leaned forward and high-fived her. "I wouldn't tell my mother, but it's even better than the desserts she makes."

"How is Mother Parker? I haven't seen her in a while."

He averted his eyes. "She's over at another church now. It's been about six months."

"Oh," was all Leah said and then turned back to the event. His mother left the church at about the same time all the drama with Solomon unfolded. So, Leah felt responsible for that. But decided to keep that information to herself.

Cory provided Leah with three separate lists of people to invite to the engagement party. "This one is from the bride. Here is the groom's list. And the final list is of investors that we want invited."

"Will I be able to contact the bride? I don't know of any woman who doesn't want to be consulted about her wedding or anything that involves it." Leah perused the list then put them in her purse.

Jeremiah and Kim are extremely busy with product development, so I'm not sure if she will have time to go over every detail with you." He picked up another file off his desk and handed it to Leah.

"Her telephone number is on the first page of the documents. Kim has provided you with information on colors, fabrics, flowers and the like. The only thing she requested is that you use the same color scheme they are using for the wedding."

Cory stood. "I apologize that our discussion has to be brief, but I have a client meeting across town." He glanced at his 18k white gold wristwatch with baguette diamonds. "I've got about thirty-five minutes to get there."

Standing, Leah said, "I can get a quote over to you this evening. But I'd be interested in knowing how many other event planners you're considering for this event."

"You're it, Leah. Your brother's reputation precedes him. So, if he says you can handle this event, that's good enough for me."

A spark of excitement. She lifted the back of her heels. Jumping a few times. "Then I've got the job. Great. I won't let you don't Cory."

"I believe you." He put on his suit jacket.

Leah glanced around his office, looking as if she was dealing with a conundrum so he asked, "Is something wrong with my office?"

"Absolutely not, it's a wonderful office. It's just that I always thought you'd become a social worker or something like that. You had such a heart for the underdog when we were younger."

He thought about her comment a moment, but just a moment. "I'll walk down with you."

"That's nice of you," she said. As they got on the elevator, she snapped her fingers. "Remember that lady you helped raise money for? The one who had been living in a battered women's shelter with her children?"

Cory nodded.

"Her oldest son just graduated college. They're doing really well. And they still attend my father's church."

"I'm glad to know that," he said and meant it.

As the elevator made it to the first floor, Leah snapped her fingers like she just remembered something, "What side of town do they want to have this party?"

He shook his head. "It won't be in Charlotte. They live in DC."

~~~

DC? How was she going to pull this off? She knew nothing about the DC area. She'd just assured Cory that she could take care of this event for him, but what if something fell through the cracks because she missed some DC detail?

She was so engrossed in her thoughts about having to plan a party in DC that she hadn't noticed the man behind her until he bumped into her.

Swinging around, Leah came face-to-face with Ned Turner. "What are you doing here?" She stepped backward, eyes growing wide like a fried egg with the yolk in the middle. "Stop stalking me!"

"I wouldn't have to stalk you if you hadn't blocked my number." He was so close that when he spewed those words, spit jutted out of his mouth and onto her cheek.

Wiping the spit from her face, she tried to keep herself from panicking. "Why are you doing this, Ned? We only went on three dates. You can't be lovesick that fast."

"I never said I was lovesick; you weren't even my first choice. But you don't get to say when our relationship ends. I'll let you know when I don't want you around anymore."

Her car was about ten steps away. She took a couple steps toward it, but he blocked her path. "I don't have time for this, Ned. You need to get over it and move on."

He grabbed her arm. "Who do you think you're talking to? You must not know about me."

"Let me go." She tried to push past him to get to her car, but Ned was too strong for her. He lunged at her and proceeded to punish her body with a series of blows. Leah cried out for help as he knocked her down to the ground and began kicking her. "Help! Please help me!" she screamed at the top of her lungs.

"No one's going to help you," he growled. "You're getting what you deserve."

As Leah faded into unconsciousness, all she remembered was Ned's menacing voice, saying she was getting what she deserved. And, in a way, she agreed with him. After all, it had been her conniving ways that had resulted in her father's heart attack. Maybe God was paying her back for the evil she had inflicted on her own family.

~ Chapter Six

She woke up in the hospital. Terrified, her eyes darted around the small room. What would she do if Ned showed up here? What if he snuck into her room and finished the job?

Leah tried to sit up, but her ribs hurt so bad she couldn't move without feeling like her body was being ripped apart. The last thing she remembered was yelling for help while Ned pummeled her to the ground.

Leah didn't know how she got to the hospital. Did Ned leave her for dead? Did a Good Samaritan rescue her? Tears rolled down her face. She touched the left side of her head, felt the bandage and the immediate shockwave of pain that exploded from that side of her head.

The door to her hospital room swung open and her mother and father rushed in with Solomon and Larissa behind them.

Alma pressed her hands against her mouth. "Oh my dear Lord, look at what that monster did to my baby."

She agreed with her mother, Ned was a monster. But how did they know about him? Leah was mortified her family knew she had dated a man like Ned Turner. They probably thought she got what she deserved, just like Ned said.

"People probably hang around that garage waiting to mug unsuspecting women." Her dad sat on the side of her bed and rubbed her right arm. The one that wasn't in a sling. "How are you feeling, sweetheart?"

Wincing, she told him, "I'm in a lot of pain, Dad. I think he broke my ribs."

Standing behind her husband, Alma said, "The doctor said your ribs are bruised, but not broken, thank God."

Solomon stood at the end of the bed, holding Larissa's hand. "Can you describe him, Sis? Officer Drake told us to call when you wake up so he can get a description of the guy."

Leah shook her head. The explosion of pain shot through it again. "I don't want to talk to anyone right now. I'm in too much pain."

"Thank God Cory was there and stopped that thief from stealing your purse," Larissa said.

"Thief? Cory?" Leah was confused. Her head felt woozy. The pain pills were beginning to kick in. All she wanted to do was sleep… sleep and not talk. She didn't want to say a word about how she got what she had coming for all her misdeeds.

Falling asleep, Leah was lulled into a sense of peace and quietness. A crazed man started chasing her. She ran like she was trying to get away from the devil and all his imps. She ran fast and so far, panting and looking back, checking that her attacker wasn't getting too close.

A cliff was ahead and she didn't see the cliff. Then she was falling, and falling. She was about to splat all over the concrete. She jerked out of her dream at the moment her face was being introduced to the ground.

Gasping for air, she lifted up and then quickly flopped back down with an, "Urgggh."

"You look like you're in a lot of pain. Do you want me to get the nurse?"

Hearing a male voice that didn't sound like one of her brothers caused Leah to grab hold of the bedrail with her free arm. She scooted as close to the railing as she could, urggh, urggh, urgghing in pain as she tried to get away from the man in her room.

"Leah, it's me, Cory. I came to check on you."

Fresh tears ran down her face. She focused on the man in front of her. "Cory?"

"Yes, it's me. Don't be afraid. I'm here with you and I told your mom that I would stay until she gets back."

His voice soothed her, calmed her. She released her grip on the bedrail. "My mother left?"

He nodded. "She went home to get a change of clothes. The nurse said she can spend the night."

Knowing that her mother was going to spend the night at the hospital with her was like finding that prized Christmas present under the tree.

Cory stepped close and wiped the tears that dampened her face. "I hate to see you like this. I wish I had caught that guy. But I was able to stop him before he hurt you anymore. And I didn't let him get away with your purse."

Closing her eyes, Leah wanted to tell Cory the truth. But he had already told her family her attacker was trying to steal her purse. If she told him the truth, he would probably think she was stupid to date a monster like Ned. "I don't even remember you being in the parking garage. I thought you were being picked up in the front of the building."

He dipped his head. "I was in the front of the building waiting on my car when I heard screaming. So, I headed to the garage, wondering if you might be in some kind of trouble."

Ned would have killed her if Cory hadn't come into the parking garage when he did. "Thank you for being there. I blacked out. Who knows what would have happened to me if you had not showed up."

Cory rubbed two fingers across his forehead. "I felt awful when I saw what that guy did to you. If I hadn't been so selfish, thinking about my business meeting, I would have walked you to your car."

"Don't." she lifted a hand. "I couldn't stand it if you blame yourself for what happened to me."

Cory's face contorted with the anger. "I'll never forget the look on that animal's face as he kicked you. He was so full of rage. I... I'm just glad I came on the scene before he could do anymore damage."

Her head started pounding again. "I don't want to talk about this anymore, if that's alright with you."

Cory sat down next to Leah's bed. "I'm sorry. I wasn't thinking. This is very traumatic for you. I should have known better than to start blubbering on about what I saw."

Since she didn't remember being kicked, Ned must have kicked her while she was down on the ground, already unconscious. What kind of a man does that? What kind of a woman dates a man who would do something like that? "I get a headache whenever I think about the attack."

"I get it." He nodded. "I need to say one thing and then I'll let it go."

She turned to face the wall, couldn't bear to see the pity in Cory's eyes one second longer. "What's that?"

"The next time a mugger tries to take your purse, just give it to him. Things can be replaced, but you can't be."

She wanted to tell Cory the truth, but the words wouldn't come. "Why do you think he was after my purse?" she asked instead.

"Because you were holding it so tight. I mean, you were unconscious, but you gripped that bag like it meant more to you than your own life."

That seemed strange to Leah because she knew that Ned wasn't trying to steal her purse. So, why was she clutching it while being attacked? But her head was too foggy to try to make sense of anything. Cory's phone started ringing. He adjusted his body on the lounge chair, but he didn't reach for his phone. "Don't you need to get that?"

"I'm here with you. Whoever it is can leave a message."

Looking out her window she could see it was dark outside. She didn't want to be alone and was thankful that Cory was with her. Cory kept trying to situate himself like he just couldn't get comfortable. "You can take one of my pillows if you want."

He waved off her suggestion. "You're the patient, Leah. Just rest. Maybe I'll ask the nurse for a blanket when she comes to check on you."

"How long do you plan to stay?"

The right side of his mouth lifted in a wry smile. "I told your family I wouldn't leave you alone. So, consider me your personal security guard until your mother gets back."

His words warmed her heart. Made her feel safe. She had been mean to Cory when they were kids, had even threatened to punch him for pulling her sister's ponytail. But by the time she became a teen and Cory was in his last year of high school, they had become friends. Or at least friends at church. But then Cory went off to college. "I haven't seen you in years, Cory. And now you're here being my hero. I appreciate it, but I know you are a very busy man."

He shook his head. "The workday is done. So, I'm not too busy to sit with an old friend."

The nurse came into the room to take Leah's vitals. The nurse glanced over at Cory, then winked at Leah. "A visit from a handsome man is all we need to make us all better, ah?" The nurse had an accent. Leah couldn't pinpoint it. Trinidad or Jamaican.

Leah glanced over at Cory. He was cheesing like somebody was about to snap his picture. "We don't want to give him the big head. So, let's just say, he's alright."

The nurse handed her the pain medication and a glass of water. "You've been doped up all afternoon, so I'm thinking you don't see too good right now."

Cory doubled over laughing. He got out of his seat and high-fived the nurse. "You told her right. That girl is too far gone on drugs to recognize a handsome man when she sees one."

If it wasn't for the pain and her whole horrible life situation in general, Leah would be laughing with Cory and the nurse because he was funny… and cute.

~ Chapter Seven

The doctor released Leah from the hospital two days later. Her mother picked her up. Leah was surprised when instead of driving her to the apartment, her mother drove to the family house. "Do you want me to wait in the car?"

Alma's head swiveled in Leah's direction. "Is something wrong with you?"

"I only asked because you stopped at the house. I figured you were picking up something before taking me to my apartment. And I wasn't sure if you wanted me going into the house or not, based on the last time I was here."

Scratching the back of her neck, Alma expelled a deep sigh. "Did you hear the doctor recommend two weeks of rest? Did you understand what he meant when he put you on blood thinners to avoid any of the bruises you received from that," her voice broke, her eyes flickered as if trying to hold back tears, "awful attack that could have killed you?"

"Yes Mama, I got what he was telling me."

"Then how could you think I would let you go back to your apartment all alone, when I know you need help? What kind of a mother would I be to abandon you at a time like this?" Alma shook her head as she got out of the car. She opened Leah's door. "I went to the store and purchased a few pairs of pajamas and under garments for you. In a few days we can go to your apartment and pick up any other items you might need."

At the mention of pjs, Leah's eyes widened as she realized she would not be in business attire, because she would not be at work for the next couple of weeks. "But Mama, I can't just lounge around in pj's for days on end. I have to get back to work or I'm going to lose the event with Cory. Then I'd have to kiss my promotion goodbye."

"Your boss was very understanding when Larissa called him," Alma said, helping Leah out of the car.

Leah scowled. "Why'd you let Larissa call my job? What did she say?"

"She told them you were in the hospital. A couple people from your job even sent flowers. I put them in your room."

Leah held on to her right arm, which was still in a sling. "Ow, ow." Ribs felt like they were being pried apart with a crowbar.

Alma reached into the back seat of the car and extracted a crutch. "I thought you would need this." She placed the crutch under Leah's left armpit. "Try walking now."

"Where'd you get this crutch?"

"We've kept them in the garage for years. Your dad used it when he sprained his ankle on the basketball court, pretending that he was Michael Jordan. He resized it to fit under your arm."

Her eyes fluttered with the memories. "That's right, I remember coming home from college for Thanksgiving and daddy was on crutches." Leah put her weight on the crutch, holding her right arm still. She hobbled toward the house, which was about twelve steps from the driveway to the front door. But it still hurt like the devil himself was poking her in the ribs.

Sucking in her breath and gritting her teeth, Leah managed to get inside the house before collapsing on the sofa.

"You just stay right there." Alma picked up the phone. "I'm going to have your brothers help me get you to your old bedroom."

"You don't have to bother them. I'm sure I'll be able to make my way down the hall with this crutch. I just need to rest a few minutes."

Alma ignored that and called the church. "Your brothers want to help you."

Leah listened as her mother requested help getting her to the bedroom. But she was sure that neither her father, nor her two brothers wanted to stop what they were doing to help her. She had wronged both her brothers and her father and now she needed their help. How pitiful was that?

Tamara had called yesterday asking if she needed to come home. Leah told her to stay where she was. She assured her sister that her wounds would heal. But Leah was beginning to wonder if all her wounds… internal and external would actually heal.

Within minutes the front door opened and her dad, Solomon and Adam entered the living room. Leah adjusted herself on the sofa and smiled at them, hoping that they would smile back. But in truth, Leah was just thankful that his evil wife, Portia wasn't with him. That woman had not only schemed to take the church away from her father, but she had almost caused her brother to be killed simply because she couldn't deal with the fact that he had gotten another woman pregnant before they were even married.

Then the front door opened again and Larissa entered with her niece, Winter Sawyer, by her side. The smile on Leah's face dropped. Winter was Adam's daughter by some woman named Summer. Leah had found out about her brother's and her father's indiscretions at about the same time, and she tried to make her father pay by using Adam's indiscretion as a pawn.

Leah was ashamed of her actions because she had schemed with Winter's mom to destroy her own father. Winter was her niece and deserved to be introduced to the family in a respectful manner. Leah felt most guilty about how she used Summer and Winter in her scheme.

"Hey Auntie Leah. How are you feeling today?" Winter asked.

The pre-teen came around the sofa and hugged her. The movement caused pain to shoot through Leah's body. But the fact that Winter wanted to hug her made the pain bearable. "I'm still a little, well, a whole lot sore. But I'm getting better. Thanks for the hug."

Adam and Solomon picked her up and carried her to the bedroom. They wanted to make sure that her arm didn't get bumped against the wall or door jam, so this journey took too good men.

Her father was right behind them. "You let us know if you need anything. I don't want you getting up for anything but going to the bathroom."

"Thank you, Dad. I'll use my cell phone to call if I need anything."

Adam handed her the TV remote and then everyone walked out of the room. As she was channel surfing, Larissa came into the room carrying a stack of books.

"I picked these up for you at the bookstore. I figured if you have to be laying around for two weeks, you might want some good mysteries to read."

Leah loved mysteries. "That was very thoughtful of you, Larissa."

"Did you see the flowers?" She pointed toward the dresser.

Leah glanced over to her dresser and there was a basket of colorful flowers and another bouquet of yellow roses. "Are those from my job?"

Larissa picked up the cards that had been attached to both sets of flowers and handed them to her. "The multicolored flowers are from several people on your job, it was signed by five different people. But the yellow roses came from a lady name Donna."

Surprise etched across Leah's face as she read the cards. "Why would Donna send me flowers? The woman doesn't even like me."

Larissa shrugged. "And just so you know," she pointed toward the room next door. "You're not the only one back home. I'll be staying in my old room too."

The thought of Larissa being here acting like the good little promised-child her parents have always wanted, rankled. It had been six months since she'd been inside her parents' home but Larissa had taken her place. With ease. "How long have you been here?" she asked, sounding accusatory. Leah caught a glimpse of sadness in Larissa's eyes and wished she could take the question back. Wished she didn't feel this way about her cousin.

"I brought my clothes over earlier today. I plan to stay so I can help take care of you," her cousin said.

"Why would you want to help me?"

"We were as thick as thieves once, Leah. I haven't forgotten. I won't abandon you in your time of need. And you wouldn't abandon me either and you know it."

Leah couldn't look at her cousin anymore. Because the truth of the matter was that she had abandoned Larissa when she had refused to help with Larissa's wedding plans. And now Larissa was moving back in to help in her time of need. Leah didn't know how to make it all make sense. She closed her eyes, feeling pain that didn't come from her bruised ribs. "I think I need to rest."

As Larissa walked out of her room, Leah had to fight back tears. It was all too much. Her family had always dismissed her. The way Leah saw it, everybody dismisses her. But now her brothers were carrying her to her room, Donna sent her flowers and Larissa was in the room next door ready to wait on her hand and foot.

Tears slid down Leah's face. Regret struck her like a lightning bolt and her heart splintered. Leah wished she could take everything back. Wished that things were different with her and her family… that they weren't just with her during her time of need, but that she could truly be a part of the Davison clan again.

Her cell phone rang. Leah didn't feel like talking to anyone, but when she glanced at the caller ID and saw that it was Cory, she accepted the call.

He greeted her and said, "I was calling to check on you. I hope you're feeling better."

Cory had come to see her two days in a row while she was in the hospital. The second night, he'd even brought popcorn and they watched a movie. "I'm doing good. My family won't allow me to do anything for myself. They are demanding that I rest."

"And you should. That guy did a number on you. And I'm hoping the description I gave the police will help them catch him real soon."

The last thing Leah wanted to do was talk about Ned while on the phone with Cory. Sighing, she said, "Me too."

"I don't want to hold you, but I was also calling to let you know I'll be meeting with another event planner tomorrow. We need to get this engagement party going for my client. It's very important and I hope you understand."

Nooo! She couldn't lose this event. Think fast... think fast. Glancing around the room, her eyes landed on those yellow roses Donna sent to her. Was Donna her answer? Would Donna do this for her?

"You don't need another event planner. My company has the best event planner on staff."

"Yes, I know that, but you're on bed rest for the next two weeks," Cory said.

"I'm good," Leah agreed, "But I work with someone who is amazing. Possibly better than I am." It hurt saying those words, but she needed this event. "Her name is Donna Phillips and I'll bring her up to speed. She can take care of getting the venue, meet with the bride-to-be and I'll work on decorations right here from my bed."

"You shouldn't have to work on anything right now."

"Cory, stop worrying about me. I need something to keep me busy while lying in bed. I can order decorations in my sleep. Just let me send Donna over tomorrow. You'll see what I'm saying. She's good."

"Sounds like a plan," he agreed. "But you're not allowed to stress over one detail about this event until you're back at work. Let your colleague take on the brunt of the work."

Exhaling with relief, Leah said, "You have my word."

~Chapter Eight

For the last three days as her family cared for her, Leah laid in her old room, thinking about that hug Winter gave her. It was an innocent hug. a hug that wasn't beguiling in the least, just an I'm-glad-to-see-you-kind of hug. Which was much appreciated, but Leah couldn't figure out why Winter was so glad to see her.

She also couldn't figure out why her mother and Larissa were constantly checking on her, bringing her food and helping her dress. And why was her father coming into her room every night to pray with her? She understood her father was a pastor and took his role seriously. But she was the daughter who had betrayed him.

Leah appreciated that her parents had allowed her to stay with them while she recuperated, but did they have to be so nice? Couldn't they let her sit in this room with a glass of water and a crust of bread? Maybe even let her smell up the room after not being helped into the shower for several days... then Leah would be able to say, she was getting what she deserved from her family. But she didn't deserve any of what they were doing.

"There's my lovely Leah." Her father entered her room with his normal warm greeting and a Bible in hand. "I just finished my online

Bible study with the men's group, and wanted to check on you before I hit the sack."

"You don't have to sit with me every night, Daddy. I know how busy you are, and I don't want to take you away from more important matters."

Bishop Davison pulled up a chair and sat next to her bed. "Please tell me who would be more important than my daughter in her time of need?"

Eyes downcast, Leah unloaded a mountain of guilt as she said, "I guess I just feel like I sorta got what I deserved and I shouldn't be getting sympathy from anyone, especially not you, Daddy."

"Oh, daughter." Bishop leaned back in his seat and looked down at the Bible in his hand. "You know, the Lord works in mysterious ways. I was going to leave my Bible in my office after my meeting, but decided I would take it with me in case I wanted to read more before falling asleep." He opened his Bible and flipped some pages. "But I think I'm going to read in here with you, if that's alright."

Leah looked at him like, do-I-have-a-choice. "It's your house, Daddy."

Bishop Davison opened his Bible to Luke, chapter fifteen. He was about to read, but then looked as if he had a better thought and handed the Bible to her. "This story is about the prodigal son. He came home to his father and asked to be treated like the servants because he didn't feel worthy. You're home now, and just like this prodigal son, you don't think you deserve to be treated like family. But here's the thing, daughter... you are and always will be family."

Leah had read the story numerous times throughout the years. But she still wasn't feeling it. "Yeah, but," Leah formed her mouth to give her father the full list of reasons why he shouldn't consider her family anymore as she took the Bible from him.

He lifted a hand. "But nothing, Leah. I could no more turn my back on you than God could turn His back on me when I fall short."

"And you still love me?" Her voice sounded timid. She had asked a question, but wasn't sure if the answer would be in her favor.

Bishop sat down on the bed next to his daughter. Looking directly at her, his eyes filling with love, he told her, "I love you all the way to the moon and back."

Her heart tightened as she heard those words… the same words he used to say when she was a kid. She remembered telling him, 'that's a lot of loving', and he had said, 'you better know it'.

Tears sprang to her eyes. She wrapped her good arm around her father. "Oh Daddy, I'm so sorry. I'm truly sorry for everything. Just please tell me that you forgive me."

Tears ran down his cheeks. He pulled out of the embrace and put Leah's hands in his. "I forgave you a long time ago. It's time for you to forgive yourself."

Her father's words hit her like lightening striking a tree. The thunderous sound of 'forgive yourself' rolled around in her ears until it got down in her soul. She wanted to forgive herself… she wanted to accept all the kindness her family had to give, but she was so ashamed of what she had done that it was easier said than done.

Her father stood and began walking out of her room. Then he paused and pointed toward the Bible. "Read that chapter."

"Okay Daddy, I will."

The next morning when she woke up, she heard noises coming from Larissa's room. She heard Larissa yell, "Just forget it, Solomon. There's no way we can make this work. We have to postpone the wedding." Then the flood of tears came.

Hearing Larissa cry like that made Leah feel like the worse cousin in the world. Why had she ignored Larissa's plea for help with planning her wedding? Leah knew how demanding Larissa's job was, after all, the girl was a doctor.

By the time Leah heard Larissa blow her nose and hiccup at the same time, she'd had enough. Leah banged her fist against the wall. "Larissa, come to my room or I'm going to hop over there on my crutch."

She heard Larissa moving around in the room, a few more sniffles, then she popped her head in Leah's room, tissue pressed against her nose. "I'm sorry if I disturbed you. Do you need me to get you anything?"

"I need you to get yourself in this room and tell me what's going on." Every night after Larissa got off work, she came home and waited on Leah like she was Florence from the Jeffersons. Leah wasn't about to see Larissa this despondent and do nothing. "Why are you crying? And why are you postponing your wedding?"

Flopping on the bed next to Leah, Larissa let out a long, dejected sigh. "It's too overwhelming for me right now. Aunt Alma has been helping me but I can't ask her to do that while she's worried about you."

Her mother was a no-nonsense, it-is-what-it-is kind of woman. Leah, rarely saw her frazzled by anything life threw at her. So, she was surprised to hear Larissa say that her mother was worried about her. "She hasn't said anything like that to me. You and that big brain of yours might be over thinking things."

Shaking her head, Larissa said, "I know her, Leah. She's worried about you. And as a doctor I'm worried also. Blood clotting can be a serious thing. So, I'm not about to ask Aunt Alma to focus on my wedding right now."

Leah was moved by her cousin's words. Larissa was willing to postpone her wedding to care for her, even after how terrible she'd been to her. Leah's eyes watered. Guilt hung on her like a heavy winter coat. "You're not postponing anything. The wedding is next month, right?"

"Yes, but the caterer cancelled, the wrong flowers were ordered and I don't have the time or the skill to put this thing together."

"Well, that's why you have me."

Larissa's eyes widened. "What?"

"You heard me. We're family. What good is having an annoying family, if we can't help each other in our time of need. Right?"

"You're not supposed to be moving around too much for another week and a half."

Leah waved her hand and pointed to the pillows under her legs. then said, "Girl please, I can put your wedding together while I lay in this bed. I'm already doing a few things for another event. Let me help out, okay?"

With a look of unease, Larissa asked, "Are you sure you want to do this?"

After all Larissa had done for her this past week and how much she was willing to give up, it made Leah sad that her cousin didn't trust her. "I'm sorry for how I've been treating you. I promise that I won't let you down."

Larissa leaned into Leah and gave her a gentle hug. She then rushed out of the room and came back holding a huge binder that held a few pages. "Here's everything I've been working on."

Taking the binder and skimming through it, Leah laughed. "You've hardly done anything. You really do need me. Especially since y'all insist on doing this quickie, shotgun wedding."

"Cookies, anyone?" Alma stood in the doorway holding a tray with fresh-out-of-the-oven chocolate chip cookies and a pot of hot tea with lemons on a saucer.

Leah dropped the wedding book onto the bed next to her and then put her hand over her face. "Mom, not your ooey, gooey, chocolate chip cookies? How much weight do you want me to gain?"

"I've got a wedding dress to fit into." Larissa held up her hands as if she was fending off a vampire trying to bite her neck.

Rolling her eyes heavenward, Alma stepped further into the room. The sweet smell of chocolate mixed with sugar and a hint of cinnamon drifted over to them. Leah and Larissa moaned like trapped animals. "You girls don't need to worry about a few extra pounds. Talk to me about weight gain when you get in your sixties. Then I might have some sympathy."

Leah took the sling off her arm and reached for the cookies. "Give them to me."

A look of alarm crossed Alma's face. "I don't think you should do that."

"My arm feels fine. And I'm tired of that sling."

Alma glanced over at Larissa.

Larissa nodded her approval. "She's worn it for five days already. It was for precautionary measure more than anything, anyway. I saw the x-ray at the hospital and the bones weren't broken. So, if her arm is feeling better, she doesn't have to wear it."

For a moment it looked like Alma was holding her breath. Then she exhaled. "Thank You, Jesus."

"Stop worrying so much, Aunt Alma. Leah is here with us. She survived that attack. And she is healing nicely."

Leah's eyes roamed from Larissa to her mother. She caught something between the two of them, like they'd been talking about her. She wondered if they knew she was lying about her attacker. But she wasn't ready to go there so she took two cookies off the tray and stuffed her mouth.

Her mother poured tea in the tea cups. "So, what are you two doing?" she asked.

Happy to make this about Larissa, rather than herself, Leah quickly said, "I'm helping this sad, sad woman with her wedding."

Larissa lowered her head. "Yes, I am sad when it comes to putting a wedding together. I admit it. I'm so thankful I will only do this once in a lifetime."

Alma smiled. "Leah is the best at handling these sorts of things." She turned to Leah. "But are you up for something like this?"

"I can make calls from my bed, Mama. And I can just use my laptop for anything else that needs to be done."

Alma pulled up a chair and rubbed her hands together. "I want to help too, I hope y'all didn't decide on anything without me. Larissa is the first girl in this family to get married and I want to be involved."

"Of course, I want your help, Aunt Alma. You're like my mother, so I don't want to do this without you." Larissa and Alma hugged.

Leah added, "You and daddy will be footing the bill, so you might as well see how much we are going to stick you with."

"Haha, very funny." Alma shook her head.

"I'm just saying… we do need that checkbook." Leah nudged Larissa. "Don't be shy girl, weddings aren't cheap. You might be a doctor, but you've got bills. And don't forget about the student loans you took out for med school." Her parents had paid for all four years for each of them but they tightened the purse strings on anything after that bachelor's degree.

"Larissa and I have already discussed a budget. I trust her to spend wisely." Alma glanced at the wedding book, then scrunched her nose. She glanced at Larissa. "You don't have much done. This wedding is in five weeks."

Larissa sounded defensive, "I have the sanctuary and the reception hall."

"Thank God your uncle is a pastor and that we turned the building behind the church into a recreational center. Or you wouldn't have either," Alma told her with a chuckle.

Leah's cell rang. She looked at the caller ID. It was Cory. She answered the phone and gave her mother and Larissa the eye. But they ignored her and just sat there, pretending to look at Larissa's hardly-anything-in-it wedding book, while they listened in on her conversation.

"You on a break?" she asked Cory.

"Taking a few minutes. I wanted to check on you. You didn't sound so good when we talked the other night."

Laughing, a little awkwardly, she told him, "That was the pain pills. But you'll be happy to know that I haven't needed any pain medication at all today."

"That's great, Leah."

He sounded so excited for her, like it mattered to him whether she got well or not. She wished she could spend all day talking to him. Hearing that baritone as he said her name. But she knew he had to get back to work and her mother and Larissa were sitting on her bed. So, she kept it business like. "Are things going well with Donna?"

"She's doing a wonderful job, but I'd like to run a few ideas by you. I could come by later, if that's okay."

Smiling into the phone, Leah assured him, "As long as it's not too late, I'm sure my parents won't mind seeing you again."

They hung up. Before Leah could even bring the subject of Cory stopping by, her mother asked, "Who was that, dear?"

As if she hadn't been listening to every word of the conversation. "It was Cory, Mom. He wants to stop by later. Is that alright with you?"

"Is it alright?" Alma hopped off the bed. "The boy was brought up in the church. He's handsome as the dickens and from what his mama told me, he's earning good money." Alma gave her daughter a quick inspection. "Let me get the hot comb and my rollers in here. I need to fix your hair."

Laughing, Leah turned to Larissa. "Can you believe her? Acting like I've got an appointment with the Queen or something."

"Girl this is better than some queen. Cory Parker is coming to see you and that brother has got it going on." Larissa took the wedding book from her. "We can look this over later. After you get out of the shower, I'm going to give you a makeover."

"You know I don't wear a bunch of makeup."

"We're not going to overdo it, just enough for Cory to see who you are, for real – for real, know what I mean?" Larissa winked at her and then left the room.

Leah leaned back against the headboard. What was supposed to be a quiet day in bed had turned into a makeover session. Leah, was happy Tamara was still in Atlanta because the former cheerleader of the family would have her practicing poses and carrying on.

~ Chapter Nine

Try as he might, Cory hadn't been able to stop thinking about Leah since he found her on the ground in the parking garage being pummeled by some lunatic.

His own cousin had been the victim of abuse so he could relate. It wasn't the I'm-trying-to-steal-your-purse type of beat down. Erlene had married a man who liked to make his point with his fist and his foot. The family begged and pleaded with Erlene to leave her abuser.

When she finally did leave, she came to stay with him for a while. Cory welcomed his cousin as his house guest and had encouraged her not to live in fear and to get out of the house and do something with her life.

That turned out to be the worst advice he could have given. Erlene took a job at a flower shop in Uptown. She loved flowers and could make things grow like nobody's business. Unfortunately, Erlene didn't get a chance to show her boss at that flower shop how much of a green thumb she had because her husband followed her from Cory's house to the flower shop, and shot Erlene and two other workers that day.

Cory had felt hollow for a long time after Erlene's death. The way Cory saw it, he had sent his cousin to her death. How does one atone for something like that?

A knock at his open door pulled Cory back to the present. His boss, R.L. McMaster was at his door and he didn't look happy. "Come in."

R.L. took the seat in front of Cory's desk. "You looked lost in thought. I almost didn't want to knock on your door when I saw the expression on your face."

I was, Cory wanted to say. But he and R.L. weren't friends. They were business associates. He didn't air his personal business at work. "I'm good, just thinking."

"Are you sure you're good?" The look on R.L's face indicated that he didn't believe him. "Because I'm getting a different vibe."

Adjusting himself in his seat, Cory straightened. "Excuse me?" R.L. was a busy man, making money and crushing it. He didn't spend a lot of time talking just to chit-chat. If he said something to you, there was a reason behind it. "Do you know something I don't?"

"I know you have an IPO closing in a month but you have been spending less time in the office lately. That's not like you. So, I've got to ask... what's going on here?"

Cory's eyebrow lifted. He bit back his annoyance. "Nothing's going on?"

"You didn't take my call a couple of days ago."

The unspoken rule at the firm was that investment bankers were always on call. Don't lose or break your phone because there were no excuses for missing a call that could make the bank millions. But Leah had needed him the other night. He saw the fear in her eyes when he walked up on her. It had brought thoughts of Erlene back to mind and how much he wished he had been there for his cousin when she needed him most. But he wasn't going to explain himself to R.L.

"The IPO for Delish Foods is moving along. We are planning an event in the next three weeks to rebuild investor confidence. The event planner I'm working with has secured the location and all of the invites are going out this week."

"Sounds good. But are you personally working with the potential investors to ensure they stay in our corner on this one? If too many investors drop out, that's game over and this IPO will be the downfall for us all."

So now R.L. felt the need to tell him how to do his job. "How many IPOs have I closed since I've been with this company, R.L.?"

R.L. stood. "No need to get your back up, Cory. The stakes are high on this one."

"Aren't the stakes high on every IPO we deliver?"

R.L. made his way to the door, but before leaving Cory's office, he said, "You're up for a promotion. Question is, how bad do you want it?"

Cory fumed inside as he watched R.L. walk away with the casual stride of a man on top of the world. How dare R.L. question his commitment to this job. He'd given this place seventy to eighty hours a week since day one. Sacrificed family and friends. He hadn't attended church in years. And he wasn't raised that way. His mother was always making sly comments about his lack of—as she put it—forsaking-to-assemble-himself.

"Marcia! Get me the investor file for Delish Foods," Cory yelled out to his assistant.

Marcia rushed into his office, holding a file while pointing at the telephone on his desk. "We're more civilized around here. I know my desk is right outside your office, but you don't have to yell. Pick up your phone and call."

Cory smiled, Marcia was the type of person who'd tell you about yourself and still expect to collect a paycheck. But she was alright with him, because she kept him organized. "I gotcha. I'm just having a day."

She handed him the file. "Boss, can I say something?"

"Can I stop you?"

She laughed. "I guess you can't." Then she laughed again like his statement had gotten funnier by the second. "But for real, don't let stuffy old R.L. McMaster get you down. I think it's good for a man to be distracted every now and again."

"What's with everybody around here? I'm not distracted." He held up the file he had requested. "I'm doing my job."

"Like I said, if she's the right one for you, there's nothing wrong with a little bit of distraction." With that Marcia went back to her desk.

"I am not distracted," Cory mumbled under his breath. He tried to concentrate on the file in front of him. But he couldn't understand why his boss thought he wasn't doing his job because he didn't take one lousy call from him. Especially since the call had been made at nine o'clock at night.

Wasn't he entitled to a life? And what was up with Marcia, laughing at him and accusing him of letting a woman distract him from making his dollars? He hadn't let anyone take his mind away from accomplishing his goal... well, since never.

Admittedly, Cory wished he hadn't pushed Erlene out of the house so soon and had been more available for his cousin. But he had been working his way up the latter and wasn't spending much time at home. He thought it would be good for Erlene to get out and do some of the things that made her happy. Seeing Leah laying on the ground, beaten like that brought back all the memories of his cousin. He was going to be there for Leah and he wasn't going to let anyone or anything stop him.

Sighing deeply, Cory's eyes watered a bit. Trying to make amends for a mistake was like trying to get out of the belly of the whale without God's help.

Cory made a few calls, chatted up a few potential investors. He then handed the Delish Foods file off to three of his team members and gave them instructions on what to do and say to each contact. About seven that evening, he called his driver. "I'm ready."

"Ready for what?" Sam asked.

"To go to the moon... what do you think? I'm ready to leave the office."

"That's interesting." Sam sounded hesitant, as if in thought, then said, "I'll be there in ten, boss."

When they hung up, Cory cleared his desk, put his laptop in his laptop bag and then slung the strap over his shoulder. As he walked toward the elevator, Cory felt eyes on him. The Junior associates acted like they were witness to a prison break, and tried their best to avert their eyes. But somehow, couldn't stop themselves from watching. Maybe they wanted to escape too.

Cory was signing off early, and didn't care what anyone had to say about it. He told Leah he would stop by to discuss the event, so he would technically still be working. But there was no way he was going to disrespect her parents by arriving at their home late into the night.

When he arrived at Leah's house, he told Sam, "Go on home, I'll get an Uber when I'm ready to leave."

Sam opened the back door to let Cory out. "Say boss, is your girl doing better?"

Sam had dropped him off at the hospital two nights in a row last week, and he had been at the office when Cory found her in the parking garage. "She's not my girl. We're old friends, and yes, she is doing better. Or at least she sounded better when I spoke to her this morning."

"Well, enjoy your evening, Mr. Parker." Sam got back in the car and waited until Cory entered the home before pulling off.

"Good evening, young man." Bishop Davison said as he opened the door.

"Not so young anymore, Pastor. But good evening. How are you doing?"

"I'm doing good. It's nice to see you again."

Cory took off his jacket as he stood in the foyer. He'd always liked Pastor Davison and thought he truly cared about the people he shepherded. When Cory had heard about the scandal of him having an outside child, and then heard that the child was actually a full-grown man, he knew Pastor Davison was the man he'd always believed him to be. He had made a mistake in his younger days.

Cory had no stones to throw at the man. "I hope I'm not visiting too late, sir."

Bishop shook his head. "If the hospitals let people slide in before eight, who am I to say different?" Bishop Davison patted him on the back and walked him toward Leah's room. "I want to thank you for what you did for Leah. It blessed my heart to know that God used someone who had been in our youth ministry to save my Leah."

They stopped in front of Leah's room. Bishop ushered him into the room and Cory sat down on the chair that was on the side of her bed. Caught off guard by Bishop's comment, he didn't say hello to

Leah who was lying in bed. He had been in the right place at the right time to save Leah. But had God truly orchestrated his movements that he was available for Leah in her time of need?

Was Leah some kind of do-over for him? He hadn't been able to save Erlene from her abuser, so had God allowed him to save Leah from a mugger? Shaking his head, Cory figured he was making more out of Bishop's statement than the man intended.

Leah waved her hands. "Hey, where'd you go?" she asked from under the covers.

Clearing his head, Cory turned to face Leah. He was immediately caught off guard by Leah and the glow of beauty emanating from her being.

She wasn't doing anything, simply, resting as the doctor required, but her hair was no longer in that dreadful ponytail. It was bouncy with curls draping the face of an angel. He was mesmerized... better yet, he could admit it, he was distracted by her beauty. And he liked it.

"You look beautiful, Leah."

She touched her hair. "Thank you."

Merriment danced in his eyes as he said, "Yeah, you told the nurse at the hospital that I was only 'alright' even though I had on one of my best suits when I visited you in the hospital. But that's okay. I'll be alright and let you be beautiful."

"If I wasn't still a little sore, I'd throw one of my pillows at you. Cause, you are not fooling me. You know how handsome you are. I'm sure women tell you that all the time."

His head turned from left to right and back again. "What women? I can assure you that there are no women hanging around just waiting to tell me how gorgeous I am."

"I didn't say gorgeous. I said handsome." She pointed a finger at him. "You're just tooting your own horn."

"If no one else is going to do it, then beep, beep."

They both laughed and then their eyes locked. He was feeling her and in more than just an I-wanna-be-your-friend kind of way. Her eyes were saying something to him as well, he just wasn't sure yet, what she was trying to communicate. He wasn't a very patient man, but he could slow his roll for Leah. He would let her recover from this awful nightmare she'd just experienced, then he would tell her all that was in his heart.

~ Chapter Ten

An entire week had passed since Leah had been in the hospital. Her ribs, although still tender, no longer felt like they were trying to cave in on her. She had taken the sling off her arm for good a few days ago.

She had worked with Larissa on her color scheme for the wedding. Larissa had chosen gray, peach and burgundy. The flowers had been ordered, as well as the decorations for the reception hall. Leah had even called Chef Darnel and asked if he would cater the reception.

To Leah's surprise, she and Chef Darnel had a pleasant conversation. He had received four major bookings from the event he catered for her and was happy to do her a favor. "Just stay out of my kitchen," he warned her.

"You won't have a problem with me. Your food is the best and I will make sure that everyone stays out of your way."

She received an email letting her know the decorations she had ordered for Larissa's wedding were on the way. Everything was going so smoothly, Leah wanted to kick herself for not helping out when she was first asked.

It was quiet in the house. Her dad was at the church working on his sermon. Larissa was at the hospital, back on shift, and her mother had left to run some errands. One of the errands involved going to Leah's apartment to get some of her clothes and hair supplies.

Since she was doing so much better and able to get around without using the crutch, it might be time to go back to her apartment. She didn't want to wear her welcome out. Maybe, she would head home this weekend and give her mom and dad back their empty nest. She was sure Larissa would go back to her apartment, once she went back to hers.

Her cell began ringing. It was her mother. The moment she answered, her mother switched to Facetime. Leah saw the frantic expression on her mother's face. "Mom, what's wrong?"

"Unless you're no longer a neat freak, then something terrible has happened."

"What?" Leah wasn't following. Her mother flipped the camera and scanned the bedroom of her apartment. The place was a total and complete mess. Her dresser drawer had been knocked over, her clothes were thrown all over the place, some of them even looked ripped. "Oh my God! Mom, get out of there!"

"I'm calling the police," her mother said.

"Why is this happening?" Leah bellowed. Tears bubbled in her eyes. It had to be Ned. She needed to come clean with the police. She had lied to her parents by allowing them to believe something that wasn't true. Leah jumped out of bed. Then touched her back as pain shot up her spine. "I'm coming down there."

"You most certainly are not. Lay back down, Leah. Don't get yourself worked up."

"But Mom, I need to see my apartment. I mean... did they take my TV?"

"No, the TV is still here. This kind of stuff happens in apartment buildings. They watch your comings and goings," Alma said.

"Someone knew you weren't at home and decided to help themselves to your valuables."

Leah wished that were true. But she wasn't sure if it was some criminal neighbor or Ned, finding one more way to terrorize her. She sat back down on her bed.

"Let me hang up with you so I can call the police. I'll be home shortly."

"Mom, be careful. Go sit in your car and wait for the police." Leah didn't want her mother trapped in that apartment with anyone who would ransack a place like that.

After they hung up, Leah wanted to call the police and tell them about Ned. But she felt trapped in this lie she was living and didn't know what to do about it. She got out of bed again and paced the floor.

The knowledge that someone had broken into her apartment made her want to climb back in bed, and get in the fetal position under her warm blanket. Life had never been this complicated when she worked for her father's ministry. Although, she wasn't blaming her mother anymore for the loss of her job, She and she alone had gotten herself fired.

Her phone rang. She thought her mom was calling back, but it was Tamara. "Hey girl," Leah said as she answered the phone.

"Do I need to come down there, Leah? What is going on?"

From her sister's tone, Leah was sure Tamara had just gotten off the phone with their mother. "No, you've got a lot going on in Atlanta. I don't need you missing work for me."

"I feel like I'm being a terrible sister."

"Larissa is here, and everybody else. There's nothing more you can do. You just got your anchor position, so how would it look if you took time off now?"

With a big, deep sigh, Tamara said, "Tell me the truth. Because I know you're not being straight with Mom and Dad. First you get beat to a pulp in some parking garage and now somebody breaks in your apartment and tore up the place. Mama says it doesn't look like anything was stolen. Your iPad and TV are still there… I might not be an investigative reporter, but I do report the news. I know when something is personal."

If Tamara had been standing in front of her, she would have seen Leah's eyes bulged out of her head like she was a cartoon character.

Leah sat down on the sofa in the living room and cried. "I don't know what to do, Sis. I'm in trouble, but I feel stuck."

"Why don't you tell somebody what's going on?"

"Because I could lose my job, Tamara. I've worked hard at this company and I'm up for a promotion."

"Tell me, Leah. If you don't spill it right now, I'm getting on a plane and flying there tonight. Then I'll let mom and dad know you're lying to them. I hope you haven't been scheming on the family again. Because I don't know how many times I can forgive that."

Leah couldn't let Tamara think she was scheming. She didn't want any more bad blood with her family, so she confessed that she knew the guy who attacked her and that she thought he might have broken into her apartment. Then swore her sister to secrecy.

"What do you mean, I can't say anything? You need help Leah."

"I know, but give me a little time. Let me decide how I want to share this news." When she and Tamara hung up, she heard a noise at the back of the house. It sounded like the trash can had fallen over. Leah jumped. Called her mother. "Are you on your way back yet?"

"No, I'm still here with the police. But your dad is on his way to check on you."

Good, because she really didn't want to be alone. The wind blew against the house. Looked like it was about to rain with how dark it was getting out there. Shivering with fear, Leah went to her bedroom, jumped in the bed, got in a fetal position and pulled the cover over her head. She cried like the rapture had occurred, and all her family had disappeared but she had been left behind.

And that was how her father found her. He pulled the cover from over her head and sat down next to her. "Don't Leah, don't do this to yourself. God will protect you, but you have to trust Him."

Leah sat up and put her arms around her father. "Oh Daddy, I'm just so afraid."

Patting her on the back, he said, "Your mother told me what happened. But there's no need for you to be worked up. Yes, someone broke into your apartment. But, thankfully, you weren't there. All the things they tore up can be replaced."

Her father was trying to get her to look on the bright side, but that was because he didn't know the whole truth. She was about to tell her father about the man who attacked her when her father got up.

His eyes were shining, looked like a light bulb had gone off in his head. "I've got something for you. I'll be right back."

While her father was in the room with her, Leah hadn't been so anxious. But the moment he left her room she felt fear creep back in.

Fear was becoming her constant friend, her roommate. It was there when she awakened every morning. Why couldn't she just tell the truth and get help? Because she was afraid of losing her job because she knew she shouldn't have dated a client... afraid of losing what little respect her family still had for her.

Leah rested her back against the headboard, brought her knees up to her chest and wrapped her arms around them. She wondered how much more Ned was planning to do to her. And when would God feel as if she'd gotten enough of what she deserved and allow her to live in peace again?

Her father returned to her bedroom with a bookmark in his hand. Sitting back on the bed beside her he said, "I have several bookmarks on certain issues that people deal with in life. Every now and again, God will direct me to give a bookmark to someone who needs it." He handed the bookmark to Leah.

At the top of the bookmark were the words, *Fear Not,* followed by ten scriptures on the bookmark. "Thank you, Daddy," she said politely. But really and truly, Leah didn't see how this was going to help her.

Her father said, "I don't just hand these bookmarks out without instructions. I don't want you putting it in your purse and forgetting about it. And I don't want you to read all the scriptures at once and think you're going to get what God wants to show you in just a few minutes."

Leah's eyebrows furrowed, giving her father an I-don't-understand glance. "Then what do you want me to do with it?"

"I want you to take your time with it. Read one scripture each day or whenever fear tries to overtake your mind. Then sit back and mediate on that scripture and ask God what He is trying to show you."

"Wow Daddy, that's deep." Leah had grown up in the church, but she was beginning to realize the church had not grown inside of her. Maybe it was time she, just like the prodigal son, accepted everything her father wanted to give her. "I can do that, Daddy."

"Let's start now." He pointed at the bookmark. "Read the first scripture you see."

Leah saw Psalm 27:1. It read:

"The Lord is my light and my salvation—whom shall I fear? The Lord is the stronghold of my life—of whom shall I be afraid?"

She read the scripture in a monotone voice. To her, it felt like just words.

"Okay, great, now we know you can read," her father said, "But do you know how to meditate on those words… how to let them get down in your spirit until they are like mm-mm good?"

Shame pricked her heart. Leah lowered her head. "No. I'm sorry, Daddy. I've heard you tell people to meditate on the Word since I was a kid, but I don't know how to do that."

"No shame in not knowing. The shame comes when we never try to figure out the things we don't know." He took her hand in his. "Do you mind if I tell you my process of meditating on the Word?"

A smile stretched across her face. "I'd love it. Please do tell."

Just like the Bible study teacher he was, her father began breaking the whole idea of meditating on the Word to her. "Let's look at this first sentence where it says, 'The Lord is the light and my salvation – whom shall I fear'. When I see the word light, I think about walking into a dark room and turning on the lights. What was dark becomes illuminated and bright. It's like God lighting my path… or Him shining a light on the truth of matters that concern me."

She was catching on, so she said. "When I read that God is my stronghold, I can meditate on the word strong. Think about how strong and powerful God is… If He is strong and powerful, then He is able to handle anything that I might be afraid of, right?"

"That's it, Leah." They high-fived. "Now, the next step is to pray about the issue. Whatever you're dealing with. Give it to God in that moment."

The door chime went off. Leah jumped as they heard a door open and close.

"It's just your Mom, I can hear her footsteps" he told her.

Alma stood in the doorway, she said, "Hello husband, hello daughter. I got everything squared away with the police. Officer McDaniel will call you if he needs any further information."

Bishop Davison stood. "Let's let Leah spend a little time with the Lord before she deals with this break-in business. I think it has overwhelmed her."

Leah nodded. For the first time in a long time, she wanted to spend some time with God so she could tell Him all about her troubles.

~~~

A few days had passed. Leah had meditated on Psalm 55:22 and Deuteronomy 31:6. She was trying to cast her cares on the Lord and she was trying to be strong and courageous. And even though the thought of going back to her apartment was terrifying, she asked her mother to stop at the apartment before they went to her doctor's appointment.

Just as she had been informed, nothing was missing. But a lot of her clothes had been ruined. She felt so violated. There was no way she'd be able to stay here and feel safe ever again. The minute her lease was up, she would be moving.

"I don't even want to be here anymore," she told her mother.

Alma nodded. "I get it. I was nineteen when I moved into my first apartment. My neighbors robbed me and I packed up and went back home to Mama."

Her mother drove her to her doctor's appointment so she could get the all clear, because she was scheduled to go back to work in a few days. After the appointment they went to the Southpark mall.

Her mother turned off the car and said, "Let's go get you some clothes."

Leah shook her head. "I don't have enough money to shop here. I need to go to T.J. Maxx or the Goodwill with the kind of budget I'm working with." The Southpark mall was the most expensive mall in Charlotte. Louis Vuitton, Gucci, Burberry, Macs, and so many other things she couldn't even afford to look at were in this mall.

"Hush, child. This shopping trip is on your daddy's credit card." Her mother giggled. "He won't know what hit him until he sees the bill."

"But—"

"Look Leah, I know that you don't have much to wear because I was in your apartment and I saw how many of your items were ripped. You're headed back to work, so we'd like to get you a few things."

Leah was still amazed whenever her mother went out of her way to do something nice for her. Yes, they were a close family. But Alma Davison didn't play. But Leah was happily coming to understand the boundless quality of her mother's forgiving nature. "To tell you the truth, Mom, I've been feeling like a total wreck lately. So, a shopping trip might be just the thing I need."

"You are not a wreck," Alma said, putting an arm around Leah as they walked into the mall. "I mean, come on—you have a good job, you're an awesome event planner. I know that because of the events you planned for the church... and, to top it off, Cory is sweet on you."

"Cory isn't sweet on me, Mama. He's just helping out an old friend. He's got too much good going on in his life to get mixed up with my drama."

They entered Nordstrom. Alma took a dress off the rack. "What do you think of this number?" Alma held up the red sleeveless floor-length dress that appeared to be quite formfitting. "Cory won't be able to resist you if you show up to that engagement party wearing this."

Leah sucked in a breath. "That is positively scandalous that you, the Bishop's wife, would suggest I wear a dress like that." Pointing at the beautiful gown, Leah added, "That 'number' is fit for an actress on the red carpet or a model on the catwalk. Not for a some event planner like me."

"That's it," Alma declared, stamping her foot. "If you put yourself down again, I'm going to make you wash out your mouth with soap. You weren't raised to think so little of yourself. You remember that, okay?"

It did seem that she had nothing but negative things to say, of late. Leah would try to rein in her words from now on. *For as he thinks in his heart, so is he... or she.* "I'm sorry for my attitude. You gave up time you could have spent with daddy or Larissa to hang out with me, and I've been nothing but miserable since we left the apartment."

Still holding the dress, Alma stepped closer to Leah and put a hand on her shoulder. "Listen to me. I'm not concerned about weather my being with you takes time away from anyone else, this is where I want to be. Right here with my daughter. I love you, Leah, and you need to accept that."

Closing her eyes, she reminded herself to believe. God loved her... her mother loved her... her family loved her. Leah took the dress. "I'm going to try this on. Thanks Mom, I've always liked your taste in clothes."

Leah stepped into the dressing room, and tried on the dress. The dress was beautiful on her. It was form fitting and hung just below her knees with a dip in the back. Stepping out of the dressing room, she felt like a fashion model as she twirled in front of her mother.

Her mother said, "You look like model. Gone girl, let me see you strut."

She strutted a few steps then stopped and blushed. "I guess red's a good color for me, huh?"

"I like it. This one's a keeper," Alma said.

Leah twirled around some more, watching her reflection in the mirror. "It sure is."

After her mother paid for the dress, the women moved on to Neiman Marcus. As they shopped, Leah and her mother carried on conversations, laughing and joking with each other. Just the way they used to when she was younger. It was weird, but even at thirty-five, Leah needed this kind of moment with her mother.

~ Chapter Eleven

Leah stood by the front glass doors of the church and watched as Cory got out of his car and strutted towards her. Good Lord that brother was fine. The way that beard etched across that redbone was a thing of beauty. She would have to remind herself to look toward the pulpit during service, because if she was looking at him, no way would she hear one word her dad had to say.

"You made it." Leah stepped back from the door as Cory entered.

Cory had called the night before, and when she told him that she was going to church he asked if he could meet her there. She hadn't wanted to admit it to her mother but she was feeling Cory Parker. He was a good guy. There was no pretense, no hidden agenda with him. And she felt safe with him.

But Cory was a very busy and important man these days. She still couldn't believe that annoying, I'm-going-to-pull-your-ponytail Cory Parker grew up to be someone others called sir or Mr. Parker because he was running things. The man was real easy on the eyes too.

He glanced at his watch. "I'm a few minutes early, right? Do we have time to see the youth room where we used to have children's church?"

"I'll take you over there after service."

He shook his head. "I've got to get to work directly after service, so I was hoping I could see it before we went into the sanctuary... for old times sakes."

"Yes, yes, of course. For old times sakes. Follow me." Her two fingers beckoned him forward.

As they walked around to the back side of the church where all of the offices and classrooms were, Leah saw Portia, Adam's wife leaning against the wall next to her brother's office. Her arms were folded across her chest and her lip was poked out. Portia couldn't stand the sight of her ever since she brought Summer, Winter's mom to their church. She didn't want Portia to say anything nasty to her in front of Cory so she rushed him past Adam's office as quickly as she could.

But she still heard Portia say, "Why is she here, Adam?"

Leah heard her brother respond, "I can't stop her from attending church. Why is this such a big deal?"

"I don't want her around my children."

Leah's eyes rolled heavenward. She knew that Portia was complaining about Winter even before she opened the door to youth church and saw her niece seated in the second row. Leah and Cory had entered the room through the back, so Winter didn't see her.

Cory was standing so close that his cologne tickled her nose. She breathed it in like it was water and she was very thirsty.

"This room seemed so much bigger when I was younger."

"I know, right," she agreed, trying to take her mind off how good he smelled.

Solomon was teaching the youth Bible class this morning. He said to the class, "Last week I asked you to pick your favorite Bible verse. So, did any of you work on this assignment?"

Most of the kids averted their heads, like they wanted to snap their fingers and become invisible. But Winter and another girl eagerly raised their hands.

"Winter," Solomon called on the girl, and then sat down as she stood up.

Winter held her Bible, flipped through a few pages and then said, "I haven't read all of the Bible yet, but the scripture I most love so far is in Genesis 50:20. It says, *'But as for you, ye thought evil against me; but God meant it unto good'*."

"Wow!" Solomon pursed his lips, stared at Winter a moment. "Such a big scripture for a young lady. Why did you pick that one?"

"The first Sunday my mom and I came to the church, my grandfather ministered from that scripture. It reminded me of Aunt Leah. She brought my mom to this church for an evil purpose, but God meant it for good. And now I have a relationship with my father, and I will always love my aunt for that."

Cory glanced at her, eyebrow raised.

"Let's go, church is starting," Leah whispered to Cory. She was so embarrassed by what Winter had said, she couldn't look him in the face. All that gorgeous and she couldn't even look at him. They sat down in the sanctuary.

Leah tried to concentrate on the sermon, but her mind kept drifting back to Winter. Her niece had been right about her. She had brought them to church for an evil purpose. Leah was thankful that things were turning out for the good for Winter. And she wanted so desperately to give her niece another hug.

"Why does it seem like you're suddenly nervous around me?" Cory asked after service as they stood together in the fellowship hall.

Leah shook her head. "I'm not, I guess I'm embarrassed by what my niece said."

"You want to talk about it?"

Cory's eyes held compassion, like he really wanted to be her shoulder to lean on. But she doubted he'd feel that way if she let him see the truth of who she was... or at least once was. Leah prayed that she was no longer that girl. She certainly didn't want to be. "Can I get a raincheck on that talk? It's still too raw for me."

"Absolutely." He hugged her and headed out the door.

Holding the door open she yelled to him, "You work too much. Do you know that? Sunday is supposed to be a day of rest."

He waved as he reached his car. "Tell my boss that. He doesn't believe in days off when we're in the middle of closing a deal."

~~~

Leah exhaled as she walked back through the doors of Events & Things. She was happy to be back at work and ready to put the final touches on the event they were doing for Cory in the next three weeks.

Her boss wouldn't let her do any more than order decorations while she was on leave, but that was okay because she was able to work with Larissa on her wedding. Leah was so happy she and her cousin were able to spend that time together. She now felt like she had her family back in her corner and that was priceless.

Adam was the only one she hadn't figured out yet. He and Portia were having marital problems and she had contributed to that problem when she brought Winter back into her brother's life. But Winter deserved her father in her life. So, Leah was sorry and not sorry about Adam's current situation.

"Hey Leah, how are you doing?" Brittany, one of her co-workers greeted her as she rounded the corner, heading to her cubicle.

"I'm doing good. I really am. Thanks for asking."

As Leah took a few more steps and was about to enter her cubicle, Brittney said, "I hope they catch that guy."

Me too. She wanted him to be brought to justice but for some other crime. Something that had nothing to do with her, so that she wouldn't be called to testify or anything. She needed a clean break. "You know what, Brittney, I'm just trying to keep calm and carry on."

"I heard that." Brittney went back to her cubicle.

Leah sat down at her desk and turned on her computer. Even though she hadn't been able to work on Cory's event, she had kept up with her emails. She was about to send Donna an email, asking her to bring all of the files for their DC event when an email from Steven, her manager, popped up.

He wanted to meet with everyone in the conference room. Leah didn't want any extra attention on her return to work. She prayed that there wasn't about to be cake and balloons in that conference room.

When she walked into the conference room, there was a cake on the table against the back wall. She lowered her head and tried to blend in with the others. This was not going to be good. She didn't want to field a bunch of questions from some well-meaning, but mostly nosey co-workers.

Steven said, "I won't keep you long, I know we all have a lot on our plates this morning. But I wanted to congratulate our newest Director of Operations and your new boss, Donna Phillips."

Hand clapping. Leah was actually hearing hand-clapping. She looked around the room and saw smiles on her co-workers faces, like they were so happy that Donna had beaten her out of the promotion Leah thought was coming her way. Especially after she landed a contracted event with C & T Capitol, one of the largest investment banks in the city, where money was flowing like honey.

Leah acknowledged that Donna had been leading the charge on that account for the past two weeks, so Ned's attack had also robbed her of this promotion. Life just wasn't fair and she wasn't in the mood to smile, congratulate and eat cake. She took her wounded feelings back to her cubicle and sulked there until Donna came to gloat. Or at least, that's the way Leah saw it.

Donna sat in the extra chair inside Leah's cubicle. "I hope there's no hard feelings, because I think you are a very talented event planner and I want us to have a good working relationship."

Was this Donna's sly way of getting Leah to bow down and kiss her ring? Uh-uh, that wasn't never going to happen. "Look Donna, we both know you got that promotion because of the client I brought to this firm. Let's not play games. You're the new director, but I want my account back, so please bring me my files and let me get to work."

"I will bring you the files," Donna said. "But I'm staying on this account. I think we will be able to bring a substantial amount of business to our firm if this event is handled right, so I'd like to schedule a meeting with you this afternoon. We can go over everything I've put together for the event."

"I don't have time for a meeting today. Just bring me the files and I'll go over them myself," Leah said.

"No." Donna was firm. "This is going to be a team effort. I'll send you a meeting invite. See you this afternoon."

Donna needed to thank Jesus that Leah had been praying with her father for the last two weeks and attended church yesterday, because everything, but the Jesus in her, wanted to snatch Donna's wig off for talking to her like that.

Donna stood and walked away like Leah didn't have a choice in whether or not they would meet. All of a sudden, Donna's word was law and she was the big dog now. The rest of them would be running behind her sniffing the polluted air.

Feeling overwhelmed, Leah took a deep breath. She continued to check her emails. She picked up the phone to call Cory and suggest that he find another agency for his client's engagement party. But that would be messy and Cory didn't deserve to be dragged into her vindictive plot for revenge.

Her eyes widened as she realized that she was thinking about revenge. But revenge for what? She couldn't go around getting back at people because she didn't get a promotion.

She just needed a moment to clear her head. Leah had witnessed firsthand the devastation being vindictive and seeking revenge caused. She once was an evildoer, yes, she could admit that. But she wasn't about that life anymore. She lowered her head and prayed, admonishing herself to think good thoughts.

Leah went into the break room, poured herself a cup of coffee, adding two sugars and a splash of cream. Inhaled... exhaled. She took a sip of her coffee and then headed back to her cubicle. She passed by the conference room, thinking about grabbing a piece of that cake to go with her coffee.

She gasped when she saw Ned Turner seated in the conference room with Brittany and Steven. Steven was at the head of the table while Ned sat next to Brittany. He whispered something in Brittany's ear and the two laughed.

Leah bolted and ran to seek refuge behind the nearest door in sight. It was a restroom—the men's, judging by the wall of urinals and the smell of urine. No matter. She entered the stall farthest from the door and closed the latch to lock herself in. She tried to take deep breaths to keep herself from hyperventilating. Tears of panic raced down her cheeks.

When she heard the restroom door swing open, she screamed.

"Leah?" Donna asked. "Are you in here? I thought I saw you come in here."

She grabbed a wad of toilet paper and started wiping her face. "Y-yes, but I'm okay. Wrong door. Silly me." Leah hoped that Donna would leave so she could regain her composure in private.

"Steven is looking for you."

"Tell him I will be there in a minute." .

"Are you sure you're okay?"

"I am," Leah lied, "No, no I'm not. I can't go into that conference room with Ned." Leah stepped out of the stall.

"What's going on?" Donna looked at Leah as if she were a troublemaker rather than a team player.

"Look, you are probably going to fire me anyway, so I may as well tell you the truth because there is no way I'm going to sit in that conference room with Ned Turner."

With furrowed brows, Donna asked, "You and Ned have issues?"

Leah's fists tightened. Fear gripped her heart. Tears started flowing again as she admitted, "He's the one who attacked me."

Donna's hand went to her mouth. Her eyes widened in horror. "Oh my God. Oh my God," Donna kept saying.

"Would you do me a favor?" Leah asked the woman whom she had been so rude to earlier.

"Yes of course, what do you need?"

"Can you grab my purse from my cubicle and bring it to me?"

Donna left out of the bathroom. When she returned, she handed Leah her purse, then said, "I am going to talk with Steven and let him know Ned will have to leave the premises at once. I suggest you contact the police."

"I will," Leah told her. Once Donna left the bathroom, Leah opened her purse and pulled out the bookmark her father had given her. The verse she read today was out of Isaiah 41:13-14. It read:

"*'For I am the Lord, your God, who takes hold of your right hand and says to you, Do not fear; I will help you. Do not be afraid, for I Myself will help you,' declares the Lord, your Redeemer, the Holy One of Israel.*"

"Forgive me, Lord," Leah said through her tears. "I have sinned against You, my family and anyone else who I thought got in my way. I don't want to be that person anymore. But I also don't want to live in fear. Help me, Lord. Remove this fear far from me."

Donna came back to the bathroom and to Leah's surprise, she told her, "Ned has left and we have informed him that Events & Things will no longer be doing business with him."

"You did that for me?"

Donna nodded. "I'm so sorry that happened to you, Leah. I really am."

Leah tried her best to hold her head up as she walked out of the men's bathroom. Her eyes were bloodshot from crying, but she held her bookmark in her hand as she went back to her desk and got to work. Next, she would figure out how to tell her family the truth and then get a restraining order.

~ Chapter Twelve

The Davison family sat around the dining room table, enjoying a simple Monday night dinner of pasta noodles with shrimp and chicken, smothered in alfredo sauce.

When they were done with the meal, Tamara glanced over at Leah, giving her a nudge to do what should have been done weeks ago.

Leah cleared her throat. "First, I want to thank you all for coming. Solomon and Adam, I know how busy you both are, so I'm not going to waste your time beating around the bush."

"What about me?" her father said. "I'm a busy man, too, you know."

Even though this was a serious moment for her, Leah appreciated her father's attempt to lighten the mood. "I know you're busy, Daddy. But you live here. So, you had no choice but to be here for me."

"I'll always be here for you, sweetheart." He winked.

Leah felt like crying. Her family truly loved her. She had been a fool, plotting and scheming. "Thank you, Daddy." She rubbed her hands together, trying to stop them from shaking. "I need to confess something to you all, because I'm at my wit's end and need help. I let you all believe that I had been attacked by a mugger and that I didn't know the man." She turned to Solomon. "You offered to help me with the case, to make sure things moved along as quickly as possible, but I didn't accept your offer because I didn't want to admit that I knew my attacker. In fact, I…I dated him."

"What?" Her father jumped out of his seat. "How long did he abuse you?"

She held up a hand. "It wasn't like that, Daddy. We only went out a few times. But it didn't take long for me to figure out that he wasn't the one for me, so I suggested we stop seeing each other. It turns out that he disagreed, and he doesn't take no for an answer. It's like he's possessed or something."

"Okay," Solomon said, taking charge. "Now we know what we're dealing with. Have you filed a restraining order?"

Leah looked away, ashamed. "No. I was trying to keep this quiet. I didn't want my boss to find out because he is, or was a client. He showed up at my job today so I had to confess that a client attacked me."

"The fear stops tonight. No job is worth this, you and I will go down to the courthouse on tomorrow morning and file the restraining order," Solomon told her.

She acquiesced. "I just want to get this over with. I don't think I'll be able to get a good night's sleep until Ned Turner is put away."

"Did you say Ned Turner?" Adam, asked, speaking for the first time since they'd gathered at the table.

Leah nodded somberly. "Do you know him?"

"He's been working on my investment strategies. He seemed like such a good guy. But I did feel uneasy when he was in my office one day and noticed the framed photo on my desk of you, Larissa, and Tamara… the way he kept looking at it seemed odd to me."

"Something is majorly wrong with him," Leah told him. "And if he knows I'm related to you, I wouldn't trust him with your finances."

"Oh, he is done," Adam said, anger flaring in his eyes.

"Good." Leah folded her arms across her chest.

But the news she'd just received was a big blow to her system. How had Ned gotten so close to her without her knowing it?

First thing Tuesday morning, Leah went with Solomon to the police station and filed a restraining order against Ned Turner. She was less than pleased, however, with the detective who'd been assigned to her case. This was the same officer who had tried to interview her when she was in the hospital.

Now, they met with him in a small conference room. After reviewing her file, the detective looked up with a frown. "I don't understand why you're asking for a restraining order if you haven't heard from this guy."

"I can't sleep, I'm nervous all the time...he came to my job on Monday," Leah explained.

"But you told us that you didn't know your attacker. Did he somehow track you because of the relationship with your brother?"

Leah shook her head. "Look, I'm sorry, but I wasn't telling the entire truth when you interviewed me in the hospital. My family was there, and I was too ashamed to admit I had dated this man."

"So, you're saying you do know him?"

"Yes. We went out about three times before I realized that he wasn't the one for me. When I tried to break things off, he started showing up at different events where he knew I'd be. He tried to attack me at an event I planned. But I got away from him, then he followed me to another client's office and attacked me there."

"And now he's working for a family member?"

"*Worked.* Past tense," Solomon interjected. "Adam is planning to end his business relationship with Mr. Turner today."

The detective looked Leah in the eyes. "I'm glad that you came forward with the truth. I can't tell you how many women I've seen end up back in the hospital, or worse, simply because they were too embarrassed to offer information that could protect them from future abuse."

After amending the police report, Leah filled out the paperwork for the restraining order.

As they left the police station, Solomon gave her a big hug. "I got your back, Sis," he reminded her. "You can stop worrying about Ned Turner. The judge will sign the temporary restraining order against him within two days."

"How temporary is this restraining order?" Leah asked, her panic rising once more.

"Calm down, Leah. Everything is a process, but we'll get through it. The temporary restraining order is valid for thirty days, because Ned has to be served and get his day in court. But you let me worry about court, because I'm going to make sure that he's hit with a restraining order that lasts at least five years. And after he is convicted and serves his time, we're going to ask for another restraining order."

~ Chapter Thirteen

Larissa's wedding was in two weeks. Leah would be in Washington, DC all next week working with Donna to put the final touches on Cory's big event for his client. So, the Davison family decided to get together to celebrate the upcoming nuptials this weekend.

Leah appreciated that the Davison clan had been willing to adjust a few dates so she could participate in the celebration. This afternoon, the women were going to a local day spa for massages and pedicures, after which they had plans to meet the men at a restaurant for dinner.

They sat in the relaxation room wearing plush white terry-cloth robes, sipping iced herbal tea while they waited for their appointments. Leah leaned back in the chair and exhaled. "I am so glad I am here with you all. My neck is so tense, I need this massage."

"Girl, who you telling?" Larissa asked. "I've had to work so many late-night shifts at the hospital I can barely function. And that's not good. My patients expect to receive quality care. I plan to compensate for my sleep deprivation by taking a nap during my massage."

Tamara yawned. "This Atlanta gig is fierce. I haven't had time off in weeks, so I'm thankful for this as well to celebrate Larissa's upcoming nuptials."

Leah's lip twisted as she nudged Tamara. "If Larissa wasn't getting married, we probably wouldn't have seen you this weekend either. You've been in Atlanta over six months now and we barely talk."

"I'm sorry about that Sis. I promise I'll do better."

Alma interjected. "And come home more often." Alma pointed a finger at Tamara. "I miss you. Just as much as I missed Leah when she wasn't coming around."

Tears flooded Leah's eyes. "I never thought I'd hear you say that you missed me not being around. Not after how things were between us."

Alma waved a hand. "Uh-uh. We're not doing this today. We are not living in the past. I'm going to enjoy all three of my daughters and let that be that."

Leah glanced over at Larissa. There was a time when Leah would have brought up that Larissa was her mother's niece, not her daughter for real. But if her mother could forgive her misdeeds, maybe it was time that she figured out a way to accept the fact that Larissa was her sister... and since she was getting ready to marry Solomon, they were sisters in more ways than one.

A masseuse came into the room and called Larissa's name.

She stood. "Time for my nap."

Leah's mother was called next, leaving Leah and Tamara alone. Tamara put down her magazine and turned to Leah. "How are you doing, really?"

Leah frowned. "What do you mean? Right now, or in general?"

"We're enjoying ourselves right now. Mama always plans wonderful events."

"She does, doesn't she?" Leah smiled. "I used to imagine I was like her...you know, moving behind the scenes, getting things done. Never needing anyone to pat her on the back. Just knowing that everyone else is happy is reward enough for her. That's why I became an event planner. I get a lot of enjoyment out of helping other people's visions become realities."

"Okay, but how are you doing?" Tamara persisted.

Leah took a deep breath. "Some days, I'm fine. I don't even think about what happened. But, by the next day, something small will happen, and I'll feel as if I'm having a panic attack. I'm constantly watching my back when I walk to my car after work."

"I'm so sorry to hear that, Sis. I've been praying you will forget everything about that awful man."

"I wish I could forget about him. That monster tried to take away my life, but I'm desperately trying to get it back."

Tamara leaned over and hugged her sister. "Just remember one thing, Leah, Trouble doesn't last for always. One of these days, he'll be behind bars, and you won't have to think about him at all."

"They have to find him first. But he can't hide forever. He has a business to run and is probably stalking other women besides me."

"I'm just thankful Solomon got involved," Tamara said. "As a lawyer he knows the system better than we do. He'll make sure the police stay on your case until they arrest that guy."

Before Leah could respond to her sister, another masseuse stepped into the room and summoned her. But, unlike Larissa, who was no doubt already asleep, Leah would likely be too tense to enjoy the full effect of her massage.

When the ladies finished with their massages they met the men at the Merrimont, a posh restaurant in uptown Charlotte. Alma had heard students from the local culinary institute would be preparing the meals that night and she wanted to try it out.

"Let's just hope they can cook," Tamara muttered as they sat down at the table.

As if she could do more than fry an egg or toast a frozen waffle, Leah thought.

"There's no way the Merrimont would allow culinary students to cook our meal unless they were star students," Adam said.

Solomon rubbed his hands together. "All I know is, I'm starving. I don't care who cooks the food, because I'm about to bash."

"He's telling the truth," Larissa told the group. "Solomon even eats my cooking with a smile on his face. He must have a rock-hard stomach."

"Just like his old man," David rubbed his stomach, grinning. He turned to Alma and added, "Of course, your meals are so good, I never have to rely on the spice of a hearty appetite."

Leah's mother grunted and eyed him as if she'd like to serve him up for dinner that night.

Everybody laughed, Leah included. She was actually having a good time.

Once the first course had been served, their father prayed over the food, and then everybody dug in. There were four courses in all: Caesar salad, cream of broccoli and cheddar soup, prime rib with garlic mashed potatoes, and, for dessert, the best banana bread pudding any of them had ever tasted.

When the server came back with the bill, their mother said, "You expect us to believe that our meal was prepared by amateur chefs?"

The server beamed. "They're talented, aren't they?"

"They cook like professional chefs," Alma affirmed. "I'd love to meet them, if at all possible."

"Let me check. I think the chef was just finishing up, so they should have time to talk." The server went into the back and returned a few minutes later. "Good news. I can take you back now."

Alma stood. She looked around at her family. "Is anyone else coming?"

They all shook their heads.

"This is all you," Tamara told her. "I'm so stuffed, I can't even move right now. We'll rest here until you get back."

"Suit yourselves. I have to meet the chef who cooked this meal."

Leah watched her mother march off toward the back of the restaurant, she felt compelled to join her. "Mama, wait up!" she called. "You never know, I might be able to use this chef for a future event."

Her mother stopped and turned with a smile. "I'm glad somebody else is as curious as I am. I'm not sure why, but I feel compelled to meet this chef who oversaw this meal." She winked at Leah. "Let's pray God makes the reason clear to me."

They followed the server to the kitchen. They weren't allowed to go inside the kitchen, so they waited just outside the doors. A young woman with the most captivating eyes and a beautiful smile stepped out.

"Chef Marla Williams," the server said to them, then turned to her. "These guests enjoyed your meal so much they requested an audience with you."

The server headed back to the dining area.

Leah's mother extended her hand to Chef Marla. "I'm Alma Davison. I simply had to let you know how thoroughly my family and I enjoyed the meal you prepared. None of us could believe that it had been made by someone still in culinary training."

"And I'm her daughter, Leah. The food was definitely some of the best I've had in a while."

Chef Marla's face glowed. "Thank you so much for the compliments, ladies. Not only am I still a student, but I attend culinary school only part-time."

"You are kidding me!" Leah's mother said. "Someone who cooks as well as you should have her own restaurant, or be one of those celebrity chefs on television."

Chef Marla laughed. "I don't know if God has that plan in store for me. At this point, I'm busy with my primary profession, and I can't give it up until He says it's time."

"And what is your primary profession?" Alma asked.

Leah only hoped her mother didn't offend the chef with her nosiness.

"I teach music at one of the local high schools," Marla said, "and I work privately with young aspiring singers on vocal performance."

"Is that so?" Alma asked, sounding intrigued. "Have you ever worked with gospel singers?"

Leah saw where this was going. The minister of music at Christ Life was moving to Los Angeles with her new husband, her mother may have just found her replacement.

Marla nodded. "Gospel is actually my preference. I used to be the minister of music at my church back home, but they couldn't afford to pay me a regular salary, so I took a teaching job out here and started culinary school shortly after. I've been here about two years now."

"Is that so?"

Leah could see the gears turning in her mother's mind. Could almost hear her silently asking God, "Is she the one? Should we pursue her as a potential replacement for the minister of music?"

Alma asked Marla for her card before she and Leah returned to their table.

"This has been a wonderful day," Alma said as the family prepared to leave. "We'll have to do this again real soon. Maybe another daughter will get married?" She scanned the table, eyes full of hope.

Out of the side of her eye, Leah saw a flash of something. She turned her head to the left and saw Ned standing about twenty feet away. He was holding something that kept flashing light in her direction. Her hand went to her heart. "Oh my God, it's him." She stood and jutted her finger toward him. "It's Ned!"

He stopped flickering the light. Leah yelled at him. "Why are you stalking me?"

Ned turned away from her and started walking to the door. Solomon, Adam and David got out of their seats and rushed to the parking lot.

Leah took out her cell phone and called the police while her mother, Tamara and Larissa headed toward the parking lot too.

Tamara grabbed Leah's hand and pulled her with them. "Come on, maybe we can beat on him before the police gets here."

But when they got outside and headed toward the parking lot, the men were walking back towards them.

"Did you catch him?" Alma asked.

David shook his head. "He took off."

Rolling her eyes, Leah said, "I'm so tired of this. I wish I'd never met that man. Honestly I don't know what's wrong with him and why he's so stuck on me. I just wish he would go find someone who wants to be bothered."

The police arrived and she gave them a description of the navy blue suit he was wearing and told them about his BMW. She prayed they would find him. But whether they did or not, she was heading to DC in the morning. At least then she would have a whole week that she didn't have to see or think about Ned Turner.

~Chapter Fourteen

Leah and Donna left for DC five days before the engagement party was to take place. The event hall manager set up a make-shift office for them so they could ensure the engagement party went off without any issues.

Steven was paying good money for their stay at the Gaylord which was in close proximity to the event hall. Even though she knew Steven would bill their client for those rooms, she still appreciated that he put them up so nicely. But she still wondered if he was waiting until this event was off the books before lowering the boom on her. She had caused the firm to lose money since they were no longer doing business with Ned. Only time would tell what would become of her position at Events & Things. Right now, she would focus on doing the best job she could so that Cory could get his promotion and bonus.

Cory was another issue. If she was being truthful with herself, she was seriously digging on him. But she couldn't afford to lose another client for her firm due to personal issues. So, when Cory arrived, she would keep it professional. Especially in front of Donna.

"Some of our boxes arrived. Do you want to go through them now or after lunch?" Donna asked.

"Might as well go through them now. That way if anything is broken, we can order a replacement."

"Good thinking." Donna and Leah headed down to the mailroom.

They found a cart, put their boxes on the cart and pushed it back to their temporary office. One by one they opened boxes filled with table favors, room decorations, centerpieces and on and on. They had two long tables brought into their office and they began sectioning off the items for where and what it would be used for.

They were making good progress but getting hungry. Donna suggested they drive over to Five Guys. They grabbed burgers and fries. As they sat at the table eating and chatting, Leah discovered Donna wasn't half bad. She was actually enjoying working with her.

For one thing, the woman knew her stuff. All of the planning for the party was spot on and exactly what Leah would have done herself. Donna had been in the event planning business longer than Leah. If Leah was being honest with herself, Donna would have beaten her out of that promotion even if she hadn't handed her one of the biggest events her company had planned all year.

"What's next, boss?"

Donna's head did a what-what. Her eyes widened as she stared at Leah. "Did you actually call me your boss?"

"Well, you are my boss, right? I might as well quit acting like a baby about it." Leah was growing up, seeing things differently. She had her father to thank for that. The weeks she spent under her parent's roof were heaven sent because it gave her a new perspective. No, she wasn't completely over the fear that gripped her heart from time to time, but the jealousy she'd been dealing with for years was beginning to fade. And oh my, my, my, what a feeling it was to be able to acknowledge someone else was good at something, probably even better at it, and not feel less than.

They went back to the office and got to work. Leah was putting together centerpieces when her cell phone rang. She didn't recognize the number. Usually, she would let the call go to voice mail, but she had been waiting on the caterer to get back with her.

"That restraining order isn't worth the paper it's written on," Ned snarled when she answered.

She dropped the phone as if it were a serpent. When she picked it back up, she double-checked the caller ID. The number was not the one she had stored in her contacts list as Ned's. She didn't know if he had borrowed someone else's phone to harass her, or if he had gotten a new phone after she'd blocked his number. But she didn't care. The restraining order stipulated he couldn't come within three hundred yards of her. Leah didn't know why this man was so fixated on her. It wasn't as if they had this great love or anything.

She hit the "end" button on her cell phone, buried it in her purse, and got back to work.

But the phone on her desk rang. As soon as she picked up, she wished she hadn't.

"How is your day going? Did you enjoy your lunch?" Ned asked.

"Why are you calling me here?"

"Why shouldn't I call you there? I want to prove to you how much I've changed. I want us to get back together."

"That will never happen." She slammed down the receiver.

When the phone started ringing again, Leah covered her face with her hands. Frustration was setting in. Ned wouldn't quit. He wasn't going to leave her alone. Would there be anywhere she could go to get away from this man?

"You want me to get that?" Donna asked.

Arms folded across her chest. "Please."

Donna brought the phone to her ear and listened for a moment. "This isn't Leah," she said. "Where did you get this number from?" He responded, then she said. "If you call here even one more time, I will notify the police. Got it?" Then she clicked the receiver back in its cradle.

"What did he say?" Leah asked.

Donna frowned. "He said you needed to watch your back."

Blowing out a sigh, Leah confessed, "I don't know what to do."

"Call the police. Report him for harassment."

"I've already filed a restraining order against him. You see what he thinks of that." Leah stared at Donna, hoping to get answers. "Did he tell you how he got this number or my cell phone number for that matter? Because I changed my number before I came back to work."

"I left our contact information with my family and with Britney because she is handling my other projects while we're in DC." She snapped her finger. "Come to think of it, Britney told me that she has known Ned for a long time. I will call the office to see if she gave him our information."

"Why would she do something like that? She knows he attacked me." Leah thought that she and Brittney were on good terms, but if she gave Ned her contact information, she would be keeping her distance from that girl.

Donna shook her head. "It sounds like you've got something on your hands. I'll be praying for you, because he needs to go on about his business."

With all these people praying for her, Leah wondered why her life kept going from bad to worse.

Donna left their office to pick up a few more boxes in the mailroom. Leah took out her bookmark and read from Psalm 118:6-7:

"The Lord is with me; I will not be afraid. What can man do to me? The Lord is with me; he is my helper."

She closed her eyes and imagined God being right there with her. If God was with her, what man would dare do her harm? Ned could sell his wolf tickets all he wanted, but the Lord Himself would protect her from that devil.

~~~

Approaching Leah's office, Cory overheard her and Donna's conversation. He couldn't help but be shocked. After what Leah had already gone through, she was dealing with some nut who was harassing her.

Cory had left work a few days early, boldly telling his boss he would be working from the DC office this week to ensure this event went smoothly. Leah and Donna had the details all planned out, but he had several meetings scheduled with potential investors. In truth, he couldn't bear the thought of Leah being so far away without him to protect her. He'd felt silly while packing his bags. But now he was glad he'd come.

He stood outside the office for a moment trying to decide if he should ask her about the phone call. She might think he was butting in where he didn't belong. Donna stepped out of the office, she turned left and headed down the hallway. She hadn't noticed him standing on the opposite side of the door.

Peeking into the office, he saw Leah had her head bowed. He heard her praying and didn't want to interrupt, so he waited. When she was done, she wiped the tears from her face.

He stepped into the office. "Anything I can do?"

Leah jumped. Hopping out of her seat, she turned toward him looking like she was ready to swing.

"It's me. Calm down."

"Cory," the word came out of her mouth like a gush of air as she sat back down. "What are you doing here? I didn't think you were coming in until Wednesday."

"I decided to pop in early. And it's a good thing I did." He nudged his head in the direction of her phone. "Do you mind telling me what that phone call was all about? And before you ask, I'm not passing out rainchecks today."

Leah leaned forward, put her head in her hands. "I don't want to drag you into this, Cory. Can you just pretend that you didn't hear any of that craziness?"

He shook his head, pulled a chair up and sat down beside her. "Don't you get it, Leah? I'm already involved. I'm in this... whatever this is, with you. So, don't tell me to just ignore it."

Sighing, she twisted her lips and looked at him. "You're right. I owe you the truth. But you're not going to like it."

"From what I heard a few minutes ago, I can almost certainly guarantee that." He scooted closer to her. "Lay it on me anyway."

"When you found me in the parking garage that day, you assumed that guy was trying to mug me. I know it was wrong, but I let you and my family continue to believe that." Exhaling, like the wind was being knocked out of her, she continued, "I know the guy who attacked me. His name is Ned Turner and we dated a few times."

Now it was Cory's turn to have the wind knocked out of him. "You dated a monster like that?"

"Don't look at me like that Cory. I didn't know he was like that. Something is wacked out about him because there is no way he should be this fixated on me."

"How many times has he beaten you?" He prayed this wasn't an Erlene situation all over again.

"It only happened once. He tried to attack me another time, but I maced him and got away. And now after I had him served with a restraining order, he called to tell me it doesn't mean anything. It's like the more I show him I don't want to be bothered with him, the more he wants me. I just don't get him."

He believed her when she told him the abuse she'd suffered at Ned's hands had been a one-time thing. He was just thankful she didn't make a habit of dating abusive men.

She was too independent and too confident for that. Back in high school, Leah had always gone her own way and done her own thing. She was nothing like his cousin, Erlene.

The world was filled with women like Erlene. He'd once witnessed a man dragging a woman by her hair into oncoming traffic. Cory and a few other bystanders had jumped out of their cars and pulled the man off her. The man told all of them to back off and then barked at his woman to "Get in the car."

Baffled, Cory had watched the woman's shoulders slacken. She had lowered her head and followed her abuser to his car. That, to him, had been the picture of insecurity: a woman who thought she was nothing without a man. A woman who needed a man to help her feel worthy as a human being.

Cory was now feeling a burden for Leah he had to protect her. He took her hand and squeezed it. "Okay, well, there has to be something else that can be done."

"I'm going to call Officer Drake and tell him about the phone call. But I doubt that they'll do anything about it. They haven't even been able to find him."

"How did he know that you were here?"

Leah lifted her hands. "Donna thinks it might have been someone we work with. But if she didn't give him our contact information, then I don't know."

Cory felt a wave of rage rise up within him. "I won't let him hurt you, Leah. Like your dad said, God sent me into that parking garage to rescue you. And I'm still here. If he calls again, I want to know about it. Okay?"

"Please stay out of this, Cory. Focus on what you have to get done this week. Like you told me, you have a lot riding on the event. Stay focused on that."

It was true that Cory was in the middle of the biggest deal of his life and didn't want to do anything to upset the process. "I have my eye on the prize. But I've got my eye on you as well. I'm going to have a talk with the owners of this event hall. I want security beefed up around here. I'll add it to the budget. And if Ned calls again, you need to inform me immediately. I'll call the police myself."

"You would do all that for me?"

"In a heartbeat," he told her. Then he walked away, pulling his cell phone out of his pocket. What Cory didn't say was that in a way, he was doing this for his cousin also. He hadn't been there for Erlene when her husband murdered her. But he wasn't going to let Leah down.

Erlene was the reason Cory had started attending youth group at Leah's church in the first place. His mom and dad had divorced, Cory had been broken up about it. Erlene and her parents had been attending Christ Life and told them about the church. He'd never told anyone about his sorrows except his youth group pastor. At that time in his life, he'd needed God's love and guidance. Even though Leah hadn't known what her friendship had meant to him at the time, Cory knew.

And he was determined not to let her suffer the same fate as his cousin.

~ Chapter Fifteen

On Friday morning, as Leah was getting into her rental car to head to the office, she noticed a piece of paper tucked beneath one of her windshield wipers. She surveyed the area to make sure she didn't see Ned hiding behind a bush. Nothing looked amiss. She grabbed the sheet of paper, got in the car, and closed the door, locking herself in.

She unfolded the paper and found a handwritten note from Ned:

I'm sorry, Leah. I will stop bothering you if you will have breakfast with me today.

Ned had followed her to DC? That's how he knew she had gotten back to the office from lunch the other day. Crumpling the note, Leah pulled out her ever-present bookmark. She had read and mediated on several of the scriptures. They were helping her to grow stronger. Today she read from Proverbs 29:25:

"Fear of man will prove to be a snare, but whoever trusts in the Lord is kept safe."

"Thank You, Jesus," she shouted into the roof of her car. "Thank You, Jesus. I don't have to be afraid of man. I trust You are able to protect me. Thank You for Your protection."

When she finished praying, Leah decided it was time for a conversation with Ned. She needed to get it through his thick head that they would never be a couple again—not that they had ever been one. She pulled her cell phone out of her purse and called him.

"You got my note?" Ned asked, his voice calm and gentle.

That was how he used to talk to her before the attack. Leah wasn't about to fall for it again. *Fool me once, shame on you. Fool me twice, then I must be a big dummy with a neon sign flashing, 'beat me'.*

"Yes, I got your note. I called to remind you about the restraining order and to tell you that I'm calling the police as soon as I hang up with you."

"Oh, that little piece of paper? Don't worry about it. The police won't enforce it if you don't call and report me."

She sucked in a deep breath, then exhaled. "Didn't you hear me. I'm calling them as soon as I hang up with YOU!" She was screaming at the top of her lungs. Taking several deep breaths, she reminded herself to calm down. "What do you want from me, Ned? Why don't we get to the bottom of all this and then go our separate ways?"

"You sound so cold. Not at all like the Leah I know and love."

She cringed. "You can't be in love with me, Ned. You barely know me. We went out a few times. That's it. There was nothing magical about it. There was nothing between us. There never will be."

"You know I love you, babe."

"Maybe you don't know what love is. A man in love wouldn't beat the object of his affections to the point where she requires hospitalization."

"I did no such thing!" he exploded.

She was tired of going through the same ol', same ol' with this man. There had to be an end. "What do you want from me?" she asked again.

"You're never coming back to me, are you?" Ned asked, using his calm tone again. He spoke as if realization had just dawned.

"There's nothing to come back to. You and I were never a couple. I hope you find a way to get that through your head."

"You're going to regret this, Leah. I promise you that." He hung up.

She hit the steering wheel and screamed out loud. She was so tired of the threats... the harassment. Her nerves were getting the best of her and she could feel a panic attack rising up. Breathe... breathe. Trouble don't last always, she told herself just as Tamara said. Life would not always be like this, and the sun will keep rising day after day.

There was a certain beauty in the sun rising just as it should. It meant God's way of ordering things was still in effect. "Order my steps, Dear Lord. Help me get through this day."

Her heavenly father had her life in His hands and she was going to be alright. She picked up her cell phone and called Officer Drake. Once she reported Ned's latest actions, she dialed her cell phone service provider, and asked them to change her number. Fifteen minutes later, after all the necessary protocol was complete, she tossed the phone back in her purse, turned on her car and drove to work.

Leah turned on the radio in an effort to get the sound of Ned's voice out of her head. Her mother always played praise CDs to soothe herself. Needing something to ease her troubled mind, Leah scanned the stations until she found one that played inspirational music. Marvin Sapp was singing "Praise Him in Advance." What struck Leah was the line about confusing the enemy with one's praise. She wondered if that was possible. Would it work on Ned? Maybe if she tried it, he would think she'd gone insane and leave her alone.

She giggled at her silly musings. But when she pulled into the parking lot at work, all her laughter dried up. Donna was standing outside the building, talking with a police officer whose squad car was parked out front.

"What's going on?" she asked Donna as she approached.

She pointed to the police car. "Check the backseat."

Ned was sitting there.

Her hand flew to her mouth. What had happened in the space of time between her hanging up from the call with Ned and her driving to work?

"I saw him sitting in his car when I arrived this morning, so I called the police," Donna told her. "They found a gun in his glove compartment."

"He came here… with a gun?" Leah started gasping for air. She had come close to meeting her end. But why had Ned invited her to breakfast if he'd been planning to kill her at her office? Her body was shaking.

Donna grabbed her arm and pulled her toward the building. "Come with me, let's get inside the building."

"Why would he want to kill me?" Her eyes were wide with fear. She was moving with Donna down the hall towards their office, but it felt like she was on one of those moving walkways that they have at Universal Studios. Like something other than herself was moving her forward, because all she wanted to do was collapse.

Donna helped her to sit down. Leah was still looking confused. Like she didn't know what, or why the world turned the way it did.

"Is it hot in here?" Sweat dripped from Leah's forehead like they were sitting in a sauna.

To Leah's surprise, Donna started crying. "I'm so sorry, Leah. I never meant for any of this to happen. Please, can you ever forgive me?"

Leah's eyebrows furrowed. Why was Donna begging for her forgiveness?

"I didn't know Ned was so disturbed. I swear to you, Leah. I didn't know. But when I called Britney last night, she admitted that she caught Ned messing with her phone the other night. She also told me that he hasn't been right since his mom left when he was a kid. He doesn't deal well with separations."

"I'm not his mama, so that shouldn't have anything to do with me."

"This is all my fault."

Leah eyes furrowed. "What are you talking about?"

Wiping the tears from her face, Donna said, "Remember the company party we had when we invited our clients and Ned came to the event?"

"Yes, of course I remember. That's where I met him."

"But what you don't know is that Ned was trying to get Brittney to leave the party with him before I stopped them."

"Wait, what? Why'd you stop him, if Brittney was who he wanted in the first place?" That's when she remembered Ned saying, 'you weren't even my first choice'. She hadn't given his words much thought, figuring he was just trying to be mean and make her feel as if she wasn't worthy of him.

"Brittney is a good event planner, but she isn't ambitious like you and I are. She wasn't my competition, but you were. I was hoping Steven would find out you were dating a client and then I'd get the promotion."

Leah was appalled by what she was hearing. "You schemed on me like that?"

Donna nodded. "It wasn't right, but my daughter is beginning college next year. My husband lost his job and, and... I was desperate." She started crying again.

But those tears didn't move Leah. "It doesn't matter who has to suffer as long as you get what you want." Leah was livid. She didn't care that Donna was now her boss. The woman was flat out wrong. And to think she had begun feeling bad about the way she had treated Donna.

"I never should have done that to you. Ever since you told me how Ned attacked you, I've been filled with so much guilt. I'm so, so sorry."

Leah popped out of her seat. "You should feel guilty, what you did was wrong." She looked this way and that, feeling all out of sorts, not knowing what to do next. Finally, she lifted the programs off her desk. "I'm taking these back to my hotel room. I'll finish putting them together there. I just can't be in the same space with you right now."

Leah was overwhelmed and outdone at the same time. She put the programs in her bag and was headed out of the building as Cory rushed in.

"What's going on? Security called and told me that a man was arrested outside the building."

She put her bags down and fell into Cory's arms. "It was Ned. He came to kill me."

Rubbing her back to comfort her, Cory said. "The police have him. And I'm here now so don't worry. Remember, I've got your back. Nothing is going to happen to you."

Cory reminded her of her brother Solomon. The brother she hadn't wanted. But these days, he was coming in handy, as Adam was busy dealing with the fallout with his wife while he struggled to give his children some sense of stability in their new reality of having an older sister.

Leah had seen firsthand how devastating the enemy's forces could be. She wouldn't allow Cory to get hurt trying to defend her. Ned was too slick and would find a way to hurt Cory if she stayed around. She came out of his embrace. "I think it's best that I go back home."

Cory put an arm around her shoulders and led her into the small conference room to the left of the front door. Then he pulled her close and wrapped his arms around her again. "You looked like you needed another hug."

She hated that he was right…and that his hug had felt so good and so right at a time in her life when everything else was so wrong. But she didn't trust her feelings or her intuition anymore. If Cory felt good and right, then he had to be all wrong for her.

She started shaking as confusion and self-doubt swept over her. How had she been so blind to Ned's nefarious ways from the start?

"Leah, calm down," Cory urged. "Why don't we sit and talk about this?"

"I—I've got to go," she stammered. "I don't want anyone else to get hurt because of the drama in my life. Especially you."

Cory took her hands in his, walked her over to the nearest chair, and helped her to sit. "That's what I want to talk to you about. I contacted the hotel and asked if they could move us into adjoining suites. You'll still have your privacy, but I'll be able to help if you need me."

"I don't want to ruin things for you, Cory."

"You're not ruining anything. The guests don't start arriving until tomorrow. Our being in connecting suites will help me sleep better."

She shouldn't leave without finishing the job. But if she was going to stay, she didn't want to be on the same floor with Donna. Didn't want to run into that woman anymore than need be. She accepted Cory's kindness. "You missed your calling in life, you know that don't you?"

His eyebrows furrowed. "What do you mean by that?"

"You were meant to be some kind of social worker... out saving the world." She shook her head. "I don't know how you ended up a banker. Every banker I've known only wanted to help himself."

"It looks like I'm helping myself as well. If this event goes well, I'll be set for life." He pointed at himself with both index fingers. "So, Robinhood, I am not."

"True that... true that." Leah couldn't believe it, but she was actually smiling. Cory was good for her in more ways than one. She was thankful Ned had been arrested, now they could just focus on the engagement / IPO party.

Back at the hotel, Leah was given keys to her new room at the front desk. Instead of being in a room with double beds, she was now staying in a suite with a living room, kitchen, bedroom and topnotch bathroom with granite on the sink and glass tile on the shower wall. This room was for millionaires. Cory was a millionaire, so it made sense he would pick rooms like this. She was sure if she opened the adjoining door to his room it would be just as nice, if not more so. The rich knew how to live.

She got to work on the programs. About halfway through she received a call from her mom and dad. She didn't want to hide anything from them, so she told them Ned had followed her to DC and had been arrested.

"I don't believe it!" her father exploded. "This is too much. Doesn't he have a job to go to?"

"I guess he had some free time and decided to use it to harass me."

Leah's mother sounded worried. "What's wrong with him? Why won't he just leave you alone?"

"He works for Satan—that's why, Mama."

"Do you think you should stay out there in DC?" her mother asked.

"You might be safer at home."

"You know what, Mom, I have decided to not let fear rule my life. You and Daddy brought us up to trust that God is able to protect us."

"I know, baby, but—"

Bishop stopped his wife in mid-sentence. "No butts about it, Alma. You heard Leah. God's got her. You and I are going to pray and get out of God's way."

Alma was silent, but just for a moment. When she finally responded, she said, "Well, let's pray now then."

And they did exactly that.

Leah hung up the phone and went back to the program booklets, because no matter how ticked off she was with Donna, the work had to get done. It took another two hours to finish the assignment. She stood to stretch. Cory knocked on the adjoining door between their rooms.

"Hey, you in there?" he asked.

"I'm here." She opened the door and Cory waved two tickets in her face. "What's that?"

"I just scored two tickets to the National Museum of African American History and Culture."

With a look of wonderment on her face, she snatched the tickets out of his hand. "Nobody I know has been able to get these tickets since they opened in September. How did you get these?"

With a tilt of his head and an impish grin, he said, "Girl, I know people. Don't play me cheap."

Stepping back and glancing down at his shoes, she said, "Ah, anybody wearing Christian Louboutin shoes is not playing cheap by any means." They were black patent leather slip-on loafers that accented his gray suit and black dress shirt. He looked like he'd been dressed by a stylist.

"Don't tell my mother how much these shoes cost, she would have a fit. 'Boy, you throwing good money away again. Don't go broke and then come ask me for rent money'," he mimicked.

She poked his shoulder with her finger. "Your mother doesn't sound like that. And anyway, she doesn't want you making foolish decisions. You're living the life most of us only dream about."

"Except I don't have a life. I'm stuck at work, grinding for my next deal, while others are having quiet dinners with their families."

She put her knuckles to her eyes as if she were drying tears. "Boohoo, the millionaire has to work while all the poor people get to play."

He laughed. "I get it. Nobody has sympathy for me. I should be grateful I earn a good living." He pointed at the tickets. "But those tickets represent the first date I've asked a woman on in at least a year, because the millionaire doesn't have time to date."

The world seemed to stand still for a moment. She stared. "You're asking me out on a date? This isn't 'take your buddy to a museum day'?"

"Leah, I'm attracted to you. I wanted to ask you out when we were in high school but you were a freshman and I was a senior. Back then the age difference seemed too wide a distance."

She was stunned. Stunned to the point where she had to remind herself to close her mouth. "And I thought you were sweet on Larissa back then. With all that hair pulling and stuff."

"Didn't you notice I only pulled her hair when you were around? I loved getting your goat. You were always defending your sisters."

She smiled, not because Cory was admitting how he felt about her, but because he called both Larissa and Tamara her sisters. Seems like everybody but her knew Larissa's true place in her life. She was going to have a heart to heart with Larissa as soon as she got back home.

"Well, since this is a date, let me change my clothes so we can get this party started."

~ Chapter Sixteen

"Wow, wow, wow," were the words floating out of Leah's mouth at every turn and every exhibit she and Cory visited at the museum. They came upon the Earl W. and Amanda Stafford Center for African American Media Arts gallery. This exhibit was called Everyday Beauty and was scheduled to be on display from September 24, 2016 until February 4, 2019.

Leah was so thankful they were able to see this exhibit in its early stages. It showcased faith, family, work, play and self-presentation of African Americans to provide positive images. The world had so depicted the African American struggle in negative ways, it was like a breath of fresh air to see the struggle from a different lens.

She and Cory viewed a series of photos from The Way of Life of the Northern Negro collection. There was a picture of a maintenance man of a railroad passenger car that had been taken in the 1940s. He was pulling a hose wrapped around his shoulders. He had on long, thick plastic gloves meant for heavy cleaning.

Cory pointed at the picture. "It is because of men like him that I am able to enjoy the lifestyle I now have. This exhibit helped me see that."

The look on Cory's face was that of a man who'd just looked into a mirror but didn't like what he saw. He took Leah's hand in his and they walked away from the exhibit. But Leah had a feeling that whatever Cory saw in that photograph… whatever meaning he took from it would stick with him for years to come.

"Let's check this exhibit out," Leah said as they came upon the A Changing America exhibit.

This exhibit was about the story of black life from 1968 and beyond. It explored social, economic, political and cultural experiences of African Americans from the untimely death of Martin Luther King, Jr. to the first and second election of former president, Barack Obama.

One of the main themes of this exhibit was to encourage visitors of the exhibit to think of ways they could help make America a more just and equitable place. Cory and Leah got the message loud and clear. It was all they could talk about over dinner.

Cory had made reservations at a seafood and steak place on Pennsylvania Ave. He ordered the seafood platter he'd ordered the three previous times he eaten at this restaurant. Leah tried the colossal crab lump cakes with a bake potato and broccoli.

"This is sooo good." Leah put another spoonful of the crab cake in her mouth. "I'm telling you, the crab meat in the Maryland/DC area must be sent down from heaven above. Because it just don't get any better than this."

During normal circumstances he would agree with her. But after viewing all of the sacrifices black people made down through the years, the scallops, lobster tail, and shrimp were wasted on him. He couldn't get the sour taste of do-nothing out of his mouth. The food went down like lead or asbestos being ripped out of an old house.

Black men and women have been in the struggle from day one, while he sat like a fat cat, getting rich and ignoring the fact that most blacks don't live like he does in this so-called land of opportunity.

"What's got you so sullen? Is something wrong with your food?"

Cory looked over at Leah. He trusted her. He didn't need to pretend everything was wonderful when he was having all these emotions. "I'm wondering about my decisions. I always imagined I would do more to help our people once I had made it. You know, like you said, I'm supposed to be saving the world or something."

Cory glanced around the high-priced restaurant. Men and women dressed to the nines were smiling and laughing over their high priced meal. They were making deals and fattening their bank accounts, but who were they helping besides themselves?

"Don't be hard on yourself, Cory. I shouldn't have suggested you were in the wrong business. I don't know why God has you at your investment firm. Only you can figure that out."

"Yeah, but who do I help? What causes do I serve other than money?"

"All those men and women we learned about chose a different path than you did. But that doesn't make what you do wrong." Leah put down her fork and reached across the table for his hand. "If you never help another soul, I'm grateful that you helped me. I wouldn't be alive if you hadn't stopped Ned from attacking me."

Leah's cell phone rang. She glanced down and twisted her lips. She shoved her phone back in her purse.

Cory straightened. "Don't tell me that was Ned."

She shook her head. "I changed my number earlier so he can't call me anymore." She gave him the new number, then said, "That was Donna. But I'm not in the mood to talk to her."

Curiosity stretched across his face. "What's up with you and Donna? When I stopped in to talk to her earlier, she looked like she had been crying."

"She ought to cry." Leah rolled her eyes. "That woman is a piece of work. Just when I was starting to think she was good people, I find out that she's been trying to sabotage me all along."

Cory put his elbows on the table and rubbed his hands together. "I'm not trying to get into your business. But from what I've seen of Donna, and how upset she was today, I think she is sorry for whatever she did."

Pointing her fork at him, she declared, "No, you are not allowed to take her side. Not today."

"I'm not taking her side, but don't you remember what your niece said about loving you even though you did something she did not like."

Please don't ask what it was, Leah screamed inside. She wasn't ready to let Cory know how much she had messed over her family. It still shocked her that they had all forgiven her.

Cory continued, "She said, that what you meant for evil, God turned it around for her good."

"I guess you shut my mouth." Leah finished her crab cake, then added, "I was so embarrassed that you heard what Winter said that day at church." She wiped her mouth with the napkin. "But I want you to know that I heard what you said, I just need some time to process it."

Cory nodded. "I get it, Leah. I'm processing some things right now as well. So, maybe we should just go through our process together." Cory tried to laugh it off, but it really was no laughing matter… his mind was turning and turning. He didn't know where he would land, but he prayed he would be right where God wanted him.

~~~

When she and Cory arrived back at the hotel, he suggested that they hang out at the pool. Leah didn't want the night to end, so she agreed, then went to her room to get ready. She had brought two swimsuits with her to DC. One was a red two-piece number that didn't leave much to the imagination. The other was an aqua, one piece her mother would approve of.

She took the aqua swimsuit inside the massive bathroom. When she emerged from the bathroom, she grabbed her beach bag, and tossed a water bottle, a novel she'd brought to read, a towel, and a small bottle of lotion inside.

Then she rummaged around in her purse for a few other items to add. As she grabbed her mints, Leah caught sight of the pepper spray she'd purchased to protect herself from Ned. She grabbed it to put it in her beach bag. But then she had a strange feeling, almost like someone whispering in her ear, telling her to put the pepper spray in the drawer of the nightstand next to her bed. Ned was in jail and she wasn't going to let him destroy her time at this beautiful hotel. She put the pepper spray in the top drawer before heading down to the pool.

~Chapter Seventeen

Down at the pool, Leah tried to concentrate on her book, but Cory was distracting her something fierce. His biceps, triceps, and washboard abs in those swim trunks were doing a number on her. She wanted to call her mother and ask for prayer to get the demon of lust off her back. Leah had been celibate since she was old enough to make that decision, and she intended to stay that way until she walked down the aisle and said "I do" to the man to whom she pledged her fidelity for life.

"Come on, Leah." Cory splashed water on her. "Put that book down and have some fun."

She couldn't be near Cory, so she said, "This book is getting good. You're the one who wanted to swim. I just need some relaxation time."

Cory got out of the pool and sauntered toward her. Water dripped off his body like summer rain on a sun-scorched beach. Leah wished for a drought. She jumped off the lounge chair. "Okay, I'll get in." She tucked her book in her beach bag, before jumping in the pool.

Cory leaped back in and the two did laps. Leah was fine with being in the pool with this gloriously built Adonis of a man as long as they were doing laps. But when they came up for air and stood within three feet of each other, she watched the water drip from his face into the pool. Leah made the mistake of looking down.

She was caught staring at his chest. Cory made his pecs do a little dance like he was Terry Crews giving out pec popping lessons.

"I've got to go back to my room." Leah got out of the pool.

"What's wrong with you?" Cory hopped out of the pool with her.

"I'll be back." She had to get away. Judging from her track record, any man to whom she was attracted ended up having a huge character flaw. As far as Leah was concerned, if she liked Cory, there was probably something wrong with him. She intended to stay as far away from him as possible. She had escaped from Ned, and now she needed to escape from Cory. Needed to run away from false love that brought her harm.

Cory caught up with her at the elevators. "Did I do something to upset you?" he asked, drying himself off with a towel.

Leah wasn't just thinking about Cory's possible character flaw. She was also thinking about her own. There were things Cory didn't know about her. She couldn't get involved with him without confessing her sins, and Leah didn't know if she was ready to do that. "No, it's not you. It's just...I need to get away."

Smiling that gorgeous grin of his, Cory said, "But you are away. Charlotte is hundreds of miles away from here."

"What I'm trying to say is, I...I've got a lot on my mind. You don't deserve having me unload on you. Not when you have a big day tomorrow."

"I have time for you, Leah. We're still on our date. Remember?"

That boyish grin of his almost did her in. But Leah wasn't so sure she had a right to be on a date with Cory. Her father always preached about getting your life in order before bringing someone else into to the hog pen with you. "I'm not the same person you used to know, Cory. I've got a lot of baggage and I don't want to disrupt your life."

Cory shook his head. He placed a hand on her arm. "I'm not letting you off the hook that easy. I saved your life, so you owe me the truth."

Leah tried to jerk away.

He put his hand around her arm again. "I get that there's bad blood between you and your family from what your niece said. But what does that have to do with us?"

He was staring at her as if he could read her very thoughts. Averting her gaze, she told him, "I'm a mess, Cory. You've got your life together. You don't need someone like me messing things up for you."

Still holding on to her arm, Cory moved them back to the pool. They sat down at one of the tables. He then extended his arm, inviting her to take the seat next to him. "No one is here but you and me. We have this whole pool area to ourselves. So, let's talk."

Propping her elbow on the table and putting a hand under her chin, Leah began, "For a long time, I felt like I was always last on my parent's list. I have come to realize how wrong I was, but that doesn't change the horrible things I did to them."

Cory's hands were placed on the table, his body language was relaxed. He didn't say anything… just waited.

It took Leah some time, but she revealed all her misdeeds. She told him how she exposed her father, for having a secret son and how she used the mother of Adam's secret daughter to blackmail her father. She even told him about her father's heart attack and how guilty she felt about that. By the time she finished Cory was scratching his head.

"I don't know what I expected. But I've got to be honest with you, Leah, I didn't expect this." He rubbed his chin. "My mother told me she had to find another church. I never asked why, but I figured it had to do with the scandal that was created when the church members found out about Solomon. I wouldn't have imagined that you orchestrated all of that against your own father. Wow."

Leah leaned back in her seat as if she'd been pushed. "I was hurt, Cory. I overreacted... not saying I'm proud of the way I reacted, but I did it and it's time I own it."

When he didn't say anything, but sat there looking shell shocked, Leah stood. "At least now you know why I'm not the person for you."

As she walked away, she fought the urge to cry. She had shed enough tears in this lifetime. She wouldn't be crying for getting rejected because of who she used to be. But she was glad that she had finally told Cory the truth. No more hiding the truth. It was time she dealt with all the confusion she had caused by being so messy for such a long time.

She thought about the forgiveness her family had bestowed on her and remembered her niece's words. Thanks to Cory bringing it up earlier, Leah realized there was someone she needed to forgive.

She got on the elevator and headed to the sixth floor. When she had left work earlier that day, she thought Donna was the worst kind of person. But after talking with Cory and seeing the look on his face, she realized that if she was willing to accept her family's forgiveness then she ought to be able to give it. She knocked on Donna's door.

Donna opened the door and Leah walked inside. The two sat—
Leah to the chair in front of the desk, and Donna with a leg tucked
under her butt at the edge of her full-sized bed.

"I'm so glad you came to see me," Donna said. "I've been
thinking and praying about what I did since you left work earlier.
And I think I should resign."

Leah hadn't expected this. She waved her hands. "Whoa, hold on
a minute. You don't need to do that."

Ringing her hands, Donna told her, "I don't want you to be
uncomfortable at work. And I'm so sorry that Ned attacked you and
is so fixated on you."

"I don't think you expected him to attack me. You need this
promotion for your child's education." Leah then grinned. "And... I
was a little obnoxious when I started at the firm." Leah could not
believe she was letting Donna off the hook so easy, but Cory was
right. What Donna meant for evil, God would turn around for her
good, she just needed to trust Him. "I'm sorry for the way I treated
you as well."

"You don't owe me an apology, Leah."

Leah stood and headed for the door. "I'll see you at work
tomorrow, boss. I need to get out of this swimsuit."

Donna followed Leah to the door. "Were you at the pool with
Cory?"

She turned getting ready to answer, but thought better of it. She
had forgiven Donna, but that didn't mean she had forgotten that this
woman had plotted to get her fired.

But Donna said, "I'm not asking as your boss. I'm not going to
tell Steven either. I just want you to be careful. Ned had been a client
of yours. How do you know Cory won't flip on you as well?"

He already had, but not in the way Donna was thinking.

~ Chapter Eighteen

To say that Cory had been caught off guard by that whole conversation with Leah, would be understating the matter. He had dated a vindictive woman before, and the situation had not ended well. Almost cost him everything.

He thought he could trust Leah; thought he knew her. So much for dating old friends. Then again, he wasn't really dating her. They had been on one date. One mind blowing date that had him rethinking his career choice and his obligations to humanity. Which was the reason he had started thinking she could be the one.

But then she ripped his guts out. All the signs were there. Leah had been abused like his cousin, Erlene. And Leah was the type of woman to plot and plan revenge just like another woman he had dated. He never should have gotten involved. He needed to get these silly high school dreams out of his head. He was a grown man. If God was flashing neon signs showing him that this woman was trouble he needed to take the hint and move on.

He would say one thing for Leah and Donna. They knew how to throw a party. Because the engagement party/investor confidence party was hitting on all cylinders. Jeremiah and Kim, the engaged couple were smiling. The investors were smiling. R.L. had given him an at-a-boy pat on the shoulder. The waiters moved through the event hall holding plates with delicious hors d'oeuvres. The guests feasted on miniature sized desserts from Delish Foods.

If all went well, the investors would pounce back on the Delish bandwagon.

Cory had dressed in his Dolce & Gabbana white linen blazer and a pair of black slacks. The ensemble was stylish without being too formal. Amid the elegant décor and romantic ambiance, Cory was all business as he shook hands and networked.

One of the investors walked over to him. "Great party, man. Thanks for inviting me. My wife can't say enough about the peach cobbler."

"Tell her to try the pound cake. That one is my favorite."

Smiling, Cory kept working the room, handling his business. Then Leah walked in and knocked him off his game with that dress. He swallowed. The form fitting red dress accentuated every curve and brought a glow to her caramel skin tone. Several men fell all over themselves in their rush to get an audience with Leah. The last thing Cory wanted to do was watch Leah prance around with a long cast of admirers all night.

Cory refused to be distracted. He got Jeremiah's attention and then signaled for the music to be turned down. He handed Jeremiah the microphone and stood next to him.

Pointing to the table that was now stacked high with small boxes bearing the Delish logo, Jeremiah said, "Kim and I are so thankful that you all could be here with us tonight to celebrate our engagement. And we don't want you to go home empty handed. So, we've brought in boxes of our bestselling peach cobbler, pound cake and our newest product, the chocolate lover's cheesecake."

Cheers went up from all around the room.

Kim strutted over and took the microphone. "Jeremiah asked me out after tasting the first chocolate cheesecake I ever made, so we thought it fitting to add it to our line of delicious treats."

It was now Cory's job to bring the soft sales pitch on home. He took the microphone and added, "Be careful who you share a piece of that cheesecake with." The group laughed. He lifted a hand to settle the group. "But seriously, can't you imagine how many millions of couples will fall in love over a piece of chocolate cheesecake or the cobbler... or my personal favorite, the pound cake? These desserts are a virtual goldmine. Each of you have the opportunity to get in on the ground floor."

On cue, Donna and Leah began passing out the program booklets to the investors.

Cory continued, "We have provided all the information you'll need to make an informed decision, but don't wait too long because this IPO goes lives in two weeks. Many of you have made a lot of money from investments that R.L. and I have sent your way. Trust me, when I tell you... the money will be flowing on this one as well."

The deejay turned up the music once Cory put down the microphone. Investors swarmed the dessert table, taking not just one of the desserts, but all three. Everybody, no matter how rich, loved to get something free. The investors left the party happy. He had done his job. Time would tell if it mattered.

Now he needed to put as much distance as possible between him and Leah. She wasn't the same girl he'd pined over since high school. With a heavy heart, he accepted that fact. He also accepted the fact that it was time to stop dreaming and to start moving forward with his life. He thought Leah would be a part of his future, but maybe he had been wrong about that.

Needing to clear his head, he stepped outside and walked around the building. Cory lifted his eyes heavenward, praying for an answer. His mother had raised him to trust God. When he was little, she would run through the house shouting praises to a God Cory couldn't see or touch. He hadn't understood it back then, but every time something good happened for their family—she got a promotion, Cory made the basketball team, they moved into a bigger house—his mother would tell him, "I prayed for that. Now I need to go thank and praise the Lord for bringing it to pass."

Right now, Cory prayed for the Lord to do something for him. He'd made tons of money. But Cory still felt as if he was in wait mode. "Can You please make it plain to me, Lord? Help me figure out what's going on with my life."

***

Alma Davison didn't know why she couldn't sleep. But an uneasy feeling had seized her and refused to let go.

She rolled over and nudged her husband. "David? You asleep?"

David only grunted.

Alma nudged him again. "Wake up."

"Huh? What's wrong?"

"I don't know," Alma told him. "But I feel like we need to pray."

"Then let's get to it." David sat up in their bed and took Alma's hands in his. Then he prayed as if lightning would strike them if they didn't call on God to move the tide of the storm. Since they didn't know which one of their children was in trouble, the Davisons prayed in tongues, believing God was well able to translate this message from the Holy Spirit and to fight this battle for them.

The Lord God Almighty was seated on His throne. The twenty-four elders surrounded Him, also seated on thrones, and clothed in radiant white robes. They wore crowns of gold on their heads.

Seven lamps of fire were burning, and a sea of crystal lay at the Masters feet. In the midst of the throne were four living creatures with eyes covering their entire bodies. The first living creature was like a lion, the second a calf, the third a man, and the fourth a flying eagle. Each of the creatures had six wings. Day and night, they moved without ceasing, soaring high above the thrones on their massive wings. Generating cool winds throughout heaven, they bellowed continuously to their King, crying, "Holy, holy, holy, Lord God Almighty, who was, and is, and is to come!"

The twenty-four elders fell down before Him and worshipped, saying, "You are worthy, O Lord, to receive glory and honor and power; for You created all things, and by Your will they exist and were created." They threw their crowns before the throne in adoration.

Then thunder rolled and lightning sparkled from the throne of grace. Michael's glorious nine-foot form stood. His colorful wings glistened as they flapped in the air. "Yes, my Lord," he said, accepting the scrolls from the Omnipotent hand that held them.

Taking his marching orders, Michael left the throne room to confer with Aaron, the captain of the host of warrior angels. As he walked through the heavens, Michael took in the beauty of it all. There were unnumbered mansions in the inner court, with room enough for everyone. But the beauty and splendor of heaven would be enjoyed only by the few who served God.

The tree of life stood, bold and beautiful, in the middle of the outer court. Its leaves were a heavenly green, and its fruit, succulent and enjoyed by all. Sweet, blissful music could be heard throughout the great expanse of heaven. It was the harp, but it was better than any harp on earth; it was the guitar, but it was better than any guitar on earth.

There were thousands upon thousands of saints moving through heaven, clothed in glistening white robes, and with bare feet. Many had crowns on their heads with various types of jewels embedded in them—jewels representing the individuals they had helped lead to Christ while on earth.

On the opposite side of the outer court stood a great multitude of warrior angels. Their appearance was that of beauty and majesty. They wore white radiant garments embellished with gold-edged trim. At the waist, each of them wore a huge golden sword, and they had large white flapping wings. The outer court was a waiting room, where saints waited for admission into the inner court and, some, to the Holy of Holies.

The warrior angels awaited their next assignments. At this moment, a great commotion stirred among the angels. He could see they were anxious—something big was about to happen—they knew it. Some asked if Michael would greet them today.

To this day, the angels remained in awe of the one angel who was able to meet Lucifer in battles and come out victorious every time. Even Gabriel had needed Michael's help when Lucifer had attacked him. They all admired their general and longed for a glimpse of him.

Captain Aaron lifted his hand, silencing the angels. "Brothers, calm yourselves. Evil is running rampant on the earth. Our general is busy putting out many fires. We do not know when he will call upon this host again, but we will be ready when he does."

Their job was to fight and destroy the works of the enemy, as God gave them leave to do so. This host of angels had won many battles and had aided numerous humans in bringing souls to the Lord.

The angels lifted their swords and shouted, "We will be ready." They were the humble elite—they got the job done.

For this reason, Michael met with their captain and provided them with as many assignments as he could. He was back today with a family they were familiar with. Michael approached the group and smiled. "Did my ears hear the sound of angels ready to do battle?"

The host of angels burst with excitement.

Captain Aaron quieted them once again. "Let's hear what the general has to say."

Michael stood in front of Aaron. Michael's sword was longer and heavier than that of the captain of the host. Jewels were embedded throughout the handle of this massive sword, a symbol of his many victories. His sword was holstered in a belt which sparkled with the gold of heaven. Michael had defeated the Prince of Persia more times than he cared to remember. But the enemy was getting stronger as his end drew near. Michael eagerly awaited their next meeting. It would be their last. "The prayers of the Davison family have risen to heaven once more," he said. "I know you lost a great number of warriors in our last battle with the wicked one. This battle will be no easier. I must know if your troops are prepared for a new battle of great magnitude."

"We are always ready, General," Captain Aaron replied. "You give the command, and we will fight until there is no more fight left in us."

"Good," Michael said, then handed him the assignment.

Captain Aaron nodded. "Consider it handled."

~Chapter Nineteen

While Cory walked outside, contemplating the possibility that he could lose in business and in love in the same weekend, an angel stood between heaven and earth, beckoning Cory to follow him.

The waters of the man-made river behind the hotel shimmered with otherworldly beauty. The array of colors blended and stretched onto a path that could lead to someplace wondrous. Cory was compelled to walk further, following the brilliant colors. "Where you lead, I will follow," he said out loud, trusting that God was listening.

~~~

Leah had seen Cory leave the party and head behind the hotel about half an hour earlier. He'd appeared to be in a foul mood, and Leah had a feeling she was responsible for it. But there was nothing she could do about that. She was human. She had made some mistakes, but she wasn't the same person anymore. Trouble was, she didn't know what type of person she was now. She felt like she was betwixt and between... like she was becoming, but still didn't know what she would become.

Cory had been good to her. He'd given her this event and had protected her from Ned. And now she had pushed him away. But she didn't regret telling him about her past. It was a part of her becoming. She didn't want to forget how horrid she had been to her family. Then she would have no reason to be thankful for how much grace they had shown her in her time of need.

"Penny for your thoughts," one of the men from the party, a potential investor said, sitting down next to her, holding two drinks in his hands. He held one out to her.

Leah stared at the glass, remembering the time right after college when the guy she was dating had tried to slip something in her drink. From that point on, Leah had made it a practice never to accept a cup if she hadn't witnessed its being filled with the contents. "No, thank you. I just drank a tall glass of iced tea."

Grinning, he said, "More for me." He took a swig of his drink, then looked into her eyes. "You're beautiful, you know that?"

Most of the time, when someone used the word "beautiful" to describe one of the Davison sisters, he was referring to Tamara or Larissa. Oh, Leah knew that she was pretty; but next to them, she just never seemed to measure up in the looks department. So, for this guy to be spouting off about how beautiful she was, Leah figured he'd probably had too much to drink. She needed to create some space between herself and one of Cory's potential investors before he started in on that second glass. She stood.

"Leaving so soon?"

She nodded. "I think I'll turn in for the night. I have a book I want to finish."

"You're going to miss all the fun."

"I've had plenty of fun already," she said with a smile, then headed back to her hotel.

***

Alma couldn't stop tossing and turning in bed.

"Still can't sleep?" David asked groggily.

She sat up, turned on the light, and grabbed his hand. "I'm worried, David. I think it Leah… Leah's in trouble."

Her husband rubbed his eyes with his free hand. "I'm sure she's fine, hon. I thought this was about Adam. He's been so down in the dumps lately that I'm really worried about him."

Alma shook her head. "It's Leah. I'm sure of it. Something has happened, David. I don't know what, but she's in trouble. We need to pray again."

David jumped out of bed and reached for the telephone. "Let's call her and see what's going on."

"Let's pray first. Then you can call."

David vacillated for a few seconds before climbing back in bed and grasping her hands once more. "Okay," he said. "I trust your discernment on this one. Let's pray."

~~~

The path Cory followed led him to a small church on the other side of the building. He hadn't attended church in a long time, but he hadn't forgotten the teachings he'd received as a youth. He'd told himself on multiple occasions that he was going to get right with God once his career was at a place where he could take time off to get his spiritual life in order.

It was late at night, but this church was rocking. The music could probably be heard more than a mile away. Cory took it as a sign that God wanted him to return to the church sooner than he'd planned. He had just been praying, asking God for help with his love life. So, he figured, why not go into this church and worship the Lord? Work on that relationship. He had no reason not to, so, he stepped inside.

The choir threw down. They sang, "Take Me to the King" and then Kirk Franklin's "I Smile." Cory was enjoying himself so much, he reached in his pocket for his cell phone, ready to call Leah and tell her to get over to this church. Then he chided himself for bringing Leah into the mix. He was having an experience with God, and Leah had nothing to do with it. He silently prayed that God would take her out of his thoughts and allow him to spend time with Him.

When the choir had finished singing, the minister, who introduced himself as Pastor Albury, stood behind the podium and offered a quick word of prayer before inviting everyone to sit. Cory prepared to hear the message, on the edge of his seat. Whenever he was in church, he never failed to receive direction for his life. He often credited his time in youth group for making him the man he was today. Cory doubted he would have been able to finish college if the youth pastor hadn't told him all those years ago that God expected him to make something of his life.

Cory was eager to hear the words that this particular preacher was about to speak into his life.

As Pastor Albury turned the pages of his Bible, he scanned the sanctuary, as if looking for someone. Once he had Cory in his sights, the preacher pointed at him. "Young man."

Cory looked around.

"You," the preacher said, still pointing at him. "Come up here, please. God has a word for you."

~~~

Still feeling awful about the way things had turned out for her and Cory, Leah put on her nightgown and sat on the edge of her bed. She pulled her cell phone out of her purse and saw that her parents had left her a voicemail. When she tried to access it, her phone powered off. Leah searched around for her charger but couldn't find it. Tucking the phone back in her purse, she picked up her novel. She would borrow Donna's charger in the morning and then give her parents a call.

She stretched out in a lounge chair on the balcony and picked up reading where she'd left off. It would be a helpful diversion—something to take her mind off the friendship she had ruined. She read for about an hour, getting all into the "boy meets girl, boy falls for girl, boy loses girl" plotline as it unfolded in the book, before her eyelids began to droop. The book was good, but she'd had an eventful day, and it was time to shut it down. She returned to her room, got ready for bed, and climbed beneath the covers before turning off the lights.

It didn't take her long to drift off. Soon, she was dreaming—about Cory's captivating smile. *They were holding hands as they walked down the street after the National Museum of African American History and Culture. When they reached the car, Cory opened the passenger door for her. Leah hesitated, then put one hand on Cory's face. She used the other to pull him closer.*

"What are you up to?" Cory asked her with a grin.

Without answering, she stood on tiptoes and brought her lips to his with a greater abandon than she'd ever exhibited. She'd had to be careful all her life, because men were always trying to take advantage of her. But the ravenous way in which Cory returned the kiss left her feeling spent and undone. They pulled apart, breaking the spell. Leah could see him, but she couldn't get to him. No matter what she did, she couldn't get around the barrier that separated them. Cory was her future, but she didn't know how to get to him.

"Calm down, baby. I'm here."

A voice penetrated her dream and caused a chill to run up her spine. She felt the covers being lifted, then someone got in the bed with her. Leah's eye darted back and forth as she racked her brain, trying to figure out how someone could have gotten into her room. She'd not only locked her door; she'd latched it, as well. Then she remembered that she hadn't locked the door to the balcony when she'd come inside from reading.

"I'm here for what you owe me."

Leah screamed, fully awake now, she jumped out of the bed. Had Ned been bailed out of jail? She hit the switch to turn on the light and faced her worst nightmare.

"Where are you going, Leah? Don't you believe in paying your debts?"

His words were slurring. "You're drunk, Ned, and I don't owe you anything." Her mind drifted back to the fear scriptures she had been reading. She remembered that Psalm 34:7 said, *the angel of the Lord encamps around those who fear Him, and He delivers them.* "Deliver me, Lord. I need Your help."

"Oh, now you want to pray." He smirked. "You weren't praying when I was spending my money on you." He reached out and grabbed her, but she pulled away.

"Get out of here." Her words were hollow, high pitched and not forceful enough to command anything.

Ned snarled, inching toward her. "Imagine my surprise when I discovered that you traveled all the way to DC to sleep with a client. When you could have just slept with me in Charlotte."

"I'm not sleeping with Cory. You're insane."

She should have been trembling with fear, but she wasn't. She knew God was on her side. He would come to her rescue. She thanked her father for teaching her that.

"I've heard from friends how Cory plans to use you and then throw you away like the trash you are."

"You're a liar!"

"How do you know?"

"I've known Cory since grade school. He's a gentleman. A decent man. He's nothing like you."

"Keep talking, and I'll smack you in that stupid mouth of yours." Ned was just inches away, ready to leap.

"Why are you still following me around if I'm trashy and stupid?" Leah demanded, running on faith-fueled adrenaline. "One would think you'd find a better way to spend your time. But you evidently have nothing better to do. Business not going so well? Is that why you have so much free time?"

He grabbed a handful of her hair and pushed her to the ground. "Say that you love me, Leah," he roared. "Tell me how much."

But Leah wasn't intimidated by him—not anymore. She shook her head. "I don't love you. I never have."

Anger etched deep furrows in Ned's face, and he slapped her. "No, Mommy. Don't talk like that. You know you love me."

Leah's head snapped back. Did he just call her mommy? Oh no, she had to make him see who she was. "I'm not your mother, Ned. It's me, Leah. Remember, you and I don't have a relationship."

"I never said you were my mother!" Ned sputtered. "I know who you are. You're the same one who tricked me into doing an event with you, to make you look good at work… and you're the same one who let me spend my money wining and dining you, and then as soon as the event was over, you wanted nothing to do with me. You women are all alike."

"I'm not your mother… you can't compare everyone to her."

"Shut up!" He shouted, putting his hands to his ears. "You can't talk to me like that."

She stood to her feet and got in his face. "Get used to it, Ned. I'm not afraid of you anymore."

"You think your lover-boy Cory Parker will keep you safe from me?" Ned reached into his jacket and pulled out a knife. "This is what I possess." He shook the weapon in her face. "And if you keep talking like that, you're going to get cut into so many pieces they'll never put you back together again."

Leah shut her mouth. But she silently prayed. Reminding God of all the ways His Word promises to protect her.

"Nothing to say, huh? You were praying earlier, but all that has gone out the window now that you see what I'm working with." He waved the knife in the air. "Go on, call out to Jesus. See if He can deliver you from my wrath."

She didn't respond but kept sending unspoken prayers heavenward.

"Go on, call Him!" he taunted her.

"My God is able to deliver me," she said. "I believe that with all my heart."

"Then you're a bigger fool than I ever imagined." He raised the knife and held it against her throat. "Aren't you?"

"No."

"You've got until the count of three to let me hear you say that you are a fool."

He started counting.

She'd felt like a fool many times in her life. Felt worthless. Like the extra child who wasn't needed. She was trying to change her perspective. But now this man was standing in front of her, trying to get her to speak ill of herself, trying to put negativity in her spirit. "Lord," she cried from the inside, "I can't believe this is what you have planned for me."

~~~

155

"How many demons are in that room with them?" Stephen asked Leon. The angels needed to get moving if they were going to save Leah.

"It's a room full of 'em. The more Leah prays, the rowdier they get. We need to do something, and fast. I'm not sure how much longer she can stand against Ned's assaults."

"We need to get Cory here so he can take care of Ned while we go to war with his demons."

"I'm on it," Leon said as he disappeared.

~ Chapter Twenty

Leon, Leah's angel, ran like the wind. His charge was in trouble, and he needed to get someone to that hotel room right now. Cory Parker was coming up the walkway to the hotel, having spent the evening slain in the spirit, hearing the words, "Come home, My son."

Cory had lain on the floor of the church and cried like he had the night he'd discovered his cousin was dead. The experiences were similar, because his spiritual life had died as well. But God was merciful. He still wanted him. Cory made up his mind that no matter what he was doing or how far he went in life, he would never forget God again.

Leon was elated for the young man's conversion experience, but now that God had gotten His business with Cory out of the way, Leon needed him to help save Leah. Waving him forward, Leon yelled out to Cory, "Something is wrong with Leah. Hurry. I heard screams coming from her hotel room."

Cory didn't ask who the man was. He sprinted into the hotel, praying she hadn't locked the door between their rooms.

Knowing the wait for the elevator would waste valuable time, Cory opted for the stairs, taking them three at a time. When he reached their floor, he opened his room with his hotel card key, while praying. "Lord, please don't let the door between our rooms be locked."

~~~

Ned ran his hand down her back.

"Don't you touch me," Leah yelled.

"That dress you wore tonight was beautiful. Did Cory buy it for you?"

"You're a pig." Wriggling to get away, Leah managed to pull one arm free of his grip. That was when she remembered the pepper spray she had tossed in the nightstand. She inched her way back towards the nightstand, reaching for it. She almost had it when Ned yanked her back toward him.

"Pig or not, you're going to give me what I came here for. Then I'll decide whether or not I'll let you keep living your miserable life."

He might have a knife, but Leah had nails. She dug her nails into his arm like she was digging for gold. He yelped, loosening his grasp enough for her to break free. She opened the drawer and grabbed the pepper spray. The next time he reached for her, she doused him. Ned screamed like he was on fire and then Leah ran into the living room, heading for the door.

"Get back here." Ned ran after her, while wiping his eyes, trying to focus. He lunged for Leah.

She reached for the doorknob but had to move the left to avoid Ned's grabby hand.

"You're not getting away from me, not this time." He lifted the knife, getting ready to attack.

The connecting door between Leah and Cory's suite burst open, and Leah swung around just in time to see Cory leap on Ned and wrestle the knife out of his hands.

"Call the police," Cory commanded.

Leah headed for the bedroom to make the call.

Ned was screaming, "I can't see. She got me with pepper spray. My eyes are burning."

"Good," Cory said.

Leah called the police and came back into the living room. He was holding the knife Ned brought to harm her, against Ned's neck. He tousled with him on the floor. "Get me something to tie his hands," Cory told Leah.

She rushed back into her bedroom and started rummaging through her suitcase. She ran back into the room and handed Cory a rope like belt that went with one of her dresses.

Cory handed Leah the knife while he tied Ned's arms.

They waited a few minutes for the police to arrive, but it seemed like hours. The police put handcuffs on Ned and took him off to jail.

Cory barked at the officers. "Can y'all not let him out this time? He stalked her with a gun in his car yesterday. Why was he let out?"

"He won't be making bond anytime soon," the officer guaranteed. They left the room.

Leah sat on the sofa, trying to settle her mind. Cory made her a cup of tea to calm her nerves. "Thank you, thank you," she gasped. "How did you know to come help me?" She couldn't stop shivering.

"I know this is going to sound crazy." He handed her the cup of tea. "But I think it was God. Or an angel. Definitely some divine nudge."

The tears that hadn't come during the attack because of the rush of adrenaline, flowed freely now. Cory sat next to her and put an arm around her shoulders. "I'm sorry about what happened to you, Leah. Do you want to talk?" he asked while handing her a Kleenex.

She took the tissue and wiped the tears from her face. "I'm so tired. When Ned started harassing me, I wondered if I was getting what I desired because of how horrible I had been to my own family.

Cory shook his head. "I'm not going to let you degrade yourself like that. Ned is sick. What he did has nothing to do with you or your family."

Leah agreed. "I realize God doesn't work like that. God forgives. He has grace for our failings. He doesn't hold it over us. He allows us to repent and then He lets us live as if it never happened."

"I learned that lesson tonight." Cory closed his eyes and took a deep breath. Then he focused on Leah. "I'm sorry for the way I responded to you last night. None of us are perfect."

"It's alright. What I did to my family was wrong." She put her feet up on the sofa and turned to him. Her eyes were still wet from crying. "But I need you to understand something. I'm not that girl anymore. These last few months have helped me to grow up."

"I believe you, Leah. I shouldn't have judged you."

Leah told him, "I'd rather be judged, than attacked or stalked by a man any day."

Cory's eyes lifted heavenward. "I just don't get that guy. Why is he so attached to you?"

Leah shrugged. "I guess I'm the kind of girl men think they can treat any kind of way. Larissa managed to find herself a man who treats her like gold, but the ones I seem to attract are snakes. The guy I dated in high school broke my heart and the guy I dated in college messed me over too. He was a cheater, and thought I should be okay with sharing him with other women."

"That's not true," Cory said with force behind his tone. "You're a woman that a man should cherish and look after."

Leah sighed. "Things would have been so different if you had been my boyfriend in high school. Maybe we would have stayed together, huh? Then I never would have taken up with Ned." She exhaled another sigh. "My list of shoulda-coulda-wouldas is so long. I'm tired of spoiling everything for everybody."

"Hey." Cory put a finger under her chin and lifted her face until she looked at him. "You're worth much more than you know. You allowed an idiot to convince you that you're worthless. But that's not true."

She tried to smile. "Thanks for saying that. Your support means a lot to me. It's encouraging that somebody believes I have changed."

"Why don't you believe in yourself? That's what I want to know."

Tears welled in her eyes. What he had said was true. She didn't think much of herself. And she hadn't for a long time. Her family was always telling her how special she was, but she couldn't stop seeing them as better than her. Why couldn't she believe in herself?

"I'm sorry," Cory said. "I didn't mean to make you cry."

She waved off his apology. "It's okay. You're right. I don't think much of myself. I keep making all the wrong choices and I'm a complete mess." She stood up and wiped the tears from her face. "I'm worn out. Do you mind if I take a shower and go back to bed?"

"Not at all. It's time for me to turn in, anyway. Call if you need anything—anything at all." He pointed toward the door that separated their room. "Leave that unlocked and I'll come running if you need me."

She said, "Thanks, Cory." She appreciated that he was right next door. But she needed him on the other side of the door, because inside, she was falling apart. His words had hit a nerve. Something had to be wrong with her. Her whole sense of self-worth was off.

When he left, Leah went into the luxurious bathroom to take a shower. She scrubbed with the aromatherapy bodywash and the loofah and she let the streaming-hot water beat and batter her body, but she still felt unclean. Cory had told her that she was worth more than she knew, but it was so hard for her to climb out of the pit she'd dug for herself. So hard for her to imagine that there could be any worth in her. So hard for her to believe that life could get better. Everywhere she turned, there was a reminder of her worthlessness.

Leah was tired of trying to change the things she couldn't change. Tired of wishing and waiting for a life she obviously couldn't have. As she got out of the shower, the phone on the nightstand rang.

"You doing okay?" Cory asked when she picked up.

"Just getting ready to lie down."

"Remember, let me know if you need anything. Oh, and one last thing."

"What is it?"

"Just making sure you know how much God loves you."

Leah didn't respond, but when she hung up, she pulled the Bible out of the drawer of her nightstand.

Thinking of how her father had asked her to meditate on those fear scriptures, she looked heavenward and said, "I need something to meditate on, Lord. Lead me to what You want me to read tonight." She began flipping pages until she stopped at Romans, chapter eight.

"There is therefore now no condemnation to them which are in Christ Jesus, who walk not after the flesh, but after the Spirit. For the law of the Spirit of life in Christ Jesus hath made me free from

the law of sin and death. For what the law could not do, in that it was weak through the flesh, God sending his own Son in the likeness of sinful flesh, and for sin, condemned sin in the flesh: that the righteousness of the law might be fulfilled in us, who walk not after the flesh, but after the Spirit."

Leah reread the words and asked herself, what it meant to her. She thought and thought about the 'there is therefore no condemnation' part. Then it hit her. "I don't have to condemn myself for the mistakes I've made."

Leah got down on her knees and prayed like she had never prayed before. Tears flowed like a river. Leah could hear music coming from Cory's side of the suite. It was CeCe Winans' "Alabaster Box.". He must be spending time in praise.

Praise Me, Leah.

She stood, but stumbled as her tears blinded her. For the first time in years, she knew without a doubt she had heard the voice of God. He wanted her to praise Him, so she lifted her hands, and sang the words to Alabaster Box.

Leah hardly recognized the feeling of worthiness, of being cherished. Yet that was how she felt, as she praised God. She felt like the Lord himself was in the room with her. She was that important to Him. "Oh, thank You, Jesus." Leah fell to the floor and continued to praise the love of her life.

~~~

In the back of the room, invisible to all human eyes, a host of angels stood watching Leah transform from the caterpillar she once was to the butterfly she would forever be—from now until eternity. They raised their swords and shouted, "Bless the Lord, for He is good!"

Then Leon smiled. His charge was finally getting it. Even though her name meant weary and tired, Leah had broken through. The weariness had left her body.

~Chapter Twenty-One

Cory rose early the next morning after spending the midnight hours in prayer for Leah. She was hurting, and he had no clue how to help her. But as he continued to pray, the Lord had brought to mind the song, Alabaster Box, he'd turned it on and then he had heard Leah singing it.

He ordered room service for breakfast, then jumped in the shower. Once the food had been delivered, Cory carried the tray and knocked on the door to Leah's suite. "Breakfast."

Leah flung open the doors. "Did someone say breakfast?"

"Have a seat." He pointed at the dining table.

Leah didn't argue. She sat and took the lid off one of the plates. "Mmm, waffles. With strawberries *and* blueberries?"

Cory shrugged. "I didn't know which topping you would prefer, so I went with both."

"Look at you, trying to make me feel all special." She smiled. Cory noticed that her lips curved all the way up, and her eyes were light with laughter.

He had recently become a firm believer in prayer. It worked—God had convinced him of that last night.

"You were blasting that praise music last night. I'm surprised no one complained about the noise."

"I heard you singing over here. So, I know you didn't call to complain." He sat and pulled a plate toward him.

"I enjoyed it. Got my breakthrough, so I'm good."

Pouring syrup on his waffles, he asked, "So, what did you have planned for the day?"

"I just want to explore the city, picking up a few souvenirs before our flight." Leah cut into her waffle.

"Sounds like fun. I was planning to go to church."

"Church? On a Saturday?"

"I found this church behind the event hall last night. They're having a revival."

Leah put down her fork and smirked. "I should have known. Of all the teens in our youth group, you seemed like the biggest church boy of them all."

"Hey, my mama raised me right. But, if I recall correctly, you and your sisters were in the youth group, too—not to mention that you were the bishop's kids."

"Okay." She grinned. "I'll admit to having had fun in youth group."

"Then come with me this morning. I know you've got your own thing planned for the day. But can you hang out with me for two hours first?" His eyes pleaded with her to say yes.

She hesitated a moment. "Oh, fine. How can I say no to a face like yours? Let's finish breakfast, and then I'll get dressed."

"Great!"

"Do you mind if I see if Donna wants to attend with us?"

"I think that would be perfect," he said as he plowed into his food.

~~~

"I can't thank you enough for bringing me to church this morning," Leah said to Cory as they headed to his rental car after the service. "I feel like God has given me a second chance. I've been born again, for real this time. It's as if all those terrible things that happened in my past didn't happen to me but to the 'me' I used to be." She twirled and danced as they made their way across the parking lot. "My parents aren't going to believe that I rededicated my life to Christ today."

"It was a beautiful service. I'm just thankful I was allowed to tag along. I needed that message today," Donna told them.

"We all needed that this morning." Cory put an arm around both ladies as they continued walking to the car. "You two put on the best engagement party I've ever attended and now I'm sharing a God moment with y'all. I'm going to make sure your firm gets more business from us."

"Now, I could shout about that." Donna did the two-step all the way to the car.

Leah and Cory laughed at her.

They got back in the car. Cory drove them to the hotel so they could pack their bags and get to the airport. Donna hopped out of the backseat and headed into the hotel. But Cory stopped Leah before she left. "I need to tell you something," he said.

She looked at him, beaming. "What is it?"

"I don't know if you have a clue about this, but I have been in love with you since we were teenagers."

Her brow furrowed in confusion. "What?"

"You heard me."

"But you never said anything back then."

"You could have waited for me to get up the nerve. But you were dating other people."

She grinned. "You were nervous? I can't believe Cory Parker was scared of a girl. You seemed very confident while you were dating half the girls in the youth choir."

"Only because I couldn't have you. None of those relationships lasted. And now I know why." He reached up and gently rubbed the side of her face. "You're the only woman for me, Leah. I want to spend the rest of my life loving you. I hope you will give me the chance."

~~~

Cory's hand felt warm and good on her face. His words had penetrated her heart with happiness. But fear crept in and stole the moment.

"Please don't do this now," Leah told him. "I have to be honest with you: Love has never been something I excelled at. Right now, the only love I can trust is the one I found with the Lord."

"You can trust me," he told her.

She closed her eyes as a tear slid down her face. "I want to trust you, Cory. I want to drop my defenses and love you with all that is in me. But I've been so wrong before…so many times."

Inching closer to her, he said, "You're not wrong about me."

Could she take a chance at love with Cory? He seemed like everything she'd ever wanted. But could she trust herself to make the right decision about a man on the heels of everything that had happened with Ned?

She needed time. Needed to pray. And she opened her mouth to tell Cory as much, but before she could utter a word, he captured her mouth with his.

The kiss was divine. It was magical. Leah didn't want it to end. But if she was ever going to have any hope of getting it right with a man, she needed to have her wits about her when she prayed. So, she moved away from the heat of his embrace. Panting, she said, "We can't."

"Please don't push me away like this," he pleaded.

"You don't have time for me, Cory. Your job is your first love. I would always come in second place. I can't live like that. I want someone who is willing to put me first, and I don't think that's too much to ask."

"What do you think I've been doing, Leah? You're the one I want. I'm ready to be what you need."

He thought he was ready. She truly wished that was the case, because she could feel her heart breaking as she tried to be strong. "Give me some time, Cory. I need to pray about this." She needed him to understand. "I know that you're a good guy. But I can't commit my heart to you unless I know you are the one God has for me."

"I understand," he said. But the look in his eyes didn't mesh with his words.

Leah touched his arm. "I meant what I said last night—that if I had dated you in high school, my life would have been a lot different. I'm tired of connecting with the wrong people and making misguided decisions about relationships. That means I need to be a lot more careful—and a lot more prayerful—with future relationships."

"I'm not going to pressure you," Cory said, holding up his hands and slowly backing away.

"Thank you, Cory. All I'm asking for is time. I want to know for sure our love is real and were not just responding to all this craziness that Ned put us through." She got out of the car and headed into the hotel to pack.

Then she remembered that she hadn't told her parents that she would be home today. She pulled her cell phone out of her purse and called her parents.

"Leah!" her mother exclaimed when she picked up. "We've been so worried about you."

"I forgot to charge my cell phone last night, Mama," she explained. "I'm sorry I didn't think to call you sooner."

"We've all been praying for you. The Lord woke me up last night. I couldn't shake the feeling that you were in grave danger," her mother told her.

Leah was thankful her parents were believers who paid attention to the things of God. Where would she be right now if they hadn't been attuned to the Spirit's guidance and hadn't prayed for her?

"I really needed those prayers, Mama," she admitted. "I'll tell you all about it when I get home this evening."

~ Chapter Twenty-Two

Back at home, Leah was excited to tell her parents about her encounter with God. She was not so excited to tell them about Ned slithering into her hotel room and trying to kill her. But it all went hand in hand, so she spilled the tea.

Alma nudged her husband. "See, I knew she had been in trouble."

"My God… to think you were in that kind of jeopardy. Makes me want to lock you in your room and never let you leave town again."

"Dad, you know better than anyone that we can't live in fear. God had me, and I'm so grateful for praying parents." Leah sat at the kitchen counter and snacked on chips while her mother made a pot of chili.

"Our little girl is growing up," Alma said to her husband.

"I am Mama," Leah said. "I went from believing in the God you serve to loving the God who first loved me. There's a world of difference between the two."

Larissa ran into the kitchen, carrying a long black garment bag. "I've got my dress. The seamstress finished the alterations."

"Well, don't keep us in suspense," Alma told Larissa. "Go put it on so we can see for ourselves."

"Okay." Grinning, Larissa turned to Leah. "Would you help me?"

"Of course." Leah followed Larissa to her room. "We don't have any time to waste so I hope this dress fits."

Larissa handed the dress bag to Leah while she took off her work clothes. "The days have gone by so fast. I can hardly believe I'll be a married woman in a week.

"That's what happens when you plan a shotgun wedding."

Larissa playfully shoved Leah's shoulder. "My man isn't being forced to marry me. He's moving halfway around the world to be with me."

Leah opened the bag and took out the dress. The bodice had hand-beaded opal and crystal stones with spaghetti straps. A silhouette of sheer material formed crisp ruffles layered from the hip line to the hem.

"This is stunning, Larissa."

"I'm glad you approve. Aunt Alma and I spent two weekends scouring dress shops until we found this one. The moment she saw it on me she started crying, so I knew this was it."

Leah's eyebrow furrowed as she lowered the dress so Larissa could step into it. "Why do you do that?" she asked.

"Do what?" Larissa pulled the spaghetti straps over her shoulder, while Leah stepped behind her to zip the back of the dress.

"Why do you call mama, Aunt Alma when she and dad adopted you at the age of twelve and you think of her as your mother?"

In slow motion, Larissa turned, turned, turned until she was facing Leah. The look on her face held every ounce of shock she must have been feeling. "Why would you ask me that? You know why."

Stepping back and giving Larissa the once over, Leah didn't answer the question. Instead, she said, "I think I just might cry myself. You look so beautiful, Larissa."

The two women hugged. Holding hands, they sat on the bed and Leah responded, "I'm the reason... I know that and I want to apologize to you."

Larissa had this I-wanna-smile-but... expression on her face. Like she didn't know whether or not to believe what she'd just heard. "Is this for real, Leah?"

Squeezing Larissa's hands, her eyes watered. "We started out as cousins, then we became best friends. When Mom and Dad adopted you, I got the best bonus of all because my cousin/best friend became my sister. But I was too jealous to accept the blessing that God had given this family. I can never make up for the years of abuse you endured from my rejecting you as a full member of this family, but I'd like to start fresh with my big sister, that is, if you even still want me to be your sister."

They were both crying now. Larissa leaned forward and pulled Leah into a big embrace. "So, I'm your big sister, huh? You're finally admitting that I'm the older girl around here?"

During their teenage years Leah and Larissa had terrible fights about who Tamara should listen to. Larissa always said, 'I'm the oldest', but Leah would counter with, 'but I'm Tamara's older sister'. She would see the hurt in Larissa's eyes, but it didn't stop her. Her mother and father had chastised her, but every now and again, she would remind Larissa that she was an outsider. "You're only older by a few months, but I'll still let you have it."

As they stood, Larissa confided, "I've been wanting to ask Aunt Alma—"

"Who?" Leah held her hand to her ear.

"I mean Mama. I've been wanting to ask Mama something, but I didn't want you to get upset so I let it go. If you're sure you're okay with me being your sister—"

Leah grabbed Larissa's hand. "Come on, you don't need my permission to ask your parents anything. Let's go to the kitchen so they can see you in this beautiful dress."

Alma and David were in deep discussion, but the moment Leah and Larissa entered the kitchen, a hush fell over the room and they just stared. Alma then turned to David, "Our girl is getting married, David. It's really happening."

"Solomon isn't go'n know what hit him when you walk down the aisle in that dress," he told Larissa.

Everyone ooohed and aaahed a little while longer, then Larissa said, "Thank you, Mom and Dad."

As Leah heard the words come out of Larissa's mouth, they felt right. Larissa was her sister and she had to share her mom and dad with her sister.

Alma burst out crying. "You called me Mom. Oh my God." She hugged Larissa. "I didn't think you'd ever feel comfortable."

"I do now." Larissa's eyes moved from David and then back to Alma. "Is it okay?"

"Are you kidding," David said, "I've always known you were my daughter. I'm thankful you now know it and want to call us Mom and Dad." He joined in on the hug.

"Awesome, because I have something else to ask." Larissa said as they came out of the embrace. Alma and David sat at the kitchen counter. Larissa leaned against the counter. "I want you both to know how much it meant to me when you not only took me in, but adopted me. I have been grateful to have you both as my parents. When I marry Solomon, I would like both my mother and father to walk me down the aisle."

"Oh my," was all Alma could say. Her hand touched her heart as she turned toward her husband."

"You heard her honey." David put an arm around Alma's shoulder. "I'm game if you are."

Alma fanned her hand in front of her face and stood. "I'm going to cry again." She hugged Larissa. "Of course, I will be there with you as you walk down the aisle." Alma then headed out of the kitchen still fanning her face.

~~~

Cory admired the floor to ceiling windows in his new fifth floor office. He had accomplished everything he'd set out to do since the day his father left him and his mother penniless and homeless. He'd been such an angry kid. Thank God he and his mother had found their way to the church.

During his time in youth church, Cory had made God promises. He'd begged God to give him the money to take care of his mother, so she didn't have to cry herself to sleep anymore. He had told God that he would help others once he had enough money to buy his mother a house.

Cory had bought his mother a house five years ago. So, what was he waiting on? How much money did he need before he would reach back and pull another brother or sister up?

R.L. waltzed into Cory's office with a box of Cuban cigars in one hand and a bottle of wine in the other. "You did it! I never should have doubted you. Delish's IPO is our biggest success yet. The partners are excited to hear what you have up your sleeve next."

Cory turned from the window and smiled at R.L. He was happy that the IPO went through. But his work here wasn't bringing him the kind of joy he now longed for. "I'm happy for you, R.L."

"I'm not just happy for me." R.L. opened the cigar box and offered one to Cory. "I'm happy for your success. Look at you... your office is now just down the hall from mine. Did you ever imagine being this successful when you first arrived at the firm?"

Cory waved off the offer of the cigar. "I don't smoke." His eyes panned the room. He took in the European Renaissance bookshelf, his massive sized mahogany desk, the sofa and overstuffed chair that had been placed to the left of his desk... to the round table that could seat four. His office was more like an Uptown apartment. And the large windows allowed him to look down on the city to see just how far he had risen.

"Tell the partners that for my next act, I will be taking a leave of absence."

The look on R.L.'s face went from joy to are-you-bat-crap-crazy. "What are you talking about? You just made twenty million dollars and you want time off? You're thinking about this all wrong, Cory. You have to keep striking while the iron is hot. If you fall back now, you may never regain the momentum you've built."

Cory shook his head. "You've been good to me, R.L. and I thank you for everything. I really do. But I'm almost forty and I don't have a family. When I die, after making all this money, who will I share it with?"

R.L.'s posture changed. For a brief moment, he no longer looked like the impressive taking-on-the-world man, Cory had modeled himself after for so long. R.L.'s shoulders slumped. "I can't help you with that. My kids don't speak to me unless they need money and my third wife is about to divorce me."

R.L. knew about making money, but he had lost the ability to function outside of his expensive office. Cory didn't want that for himself. He wanted to live, be and do everything God desired for him. He was ready to start the next chapter in his life.

~Chapter Twenty-Three

Solomon and Larissa's wedding was beautiful. Leah was the maid of honor and Tamara had come home for the weekend to be a bridesmaid along with one of Larissa's college roommates.

Two of Solomon's frat brothers came to town to serve as his groomsmen. He had asked Adam to be his best man. And just as Larissa wished, her parents walked her down the aisle to be joined with her groom.

Leah had cried more than the bride, filled with joy for Larissa and Solomon. They had found love and they would wake up in the morning in each other's arms. They would go off to work knowing that when they arrived back home, that special someone would be there with them.

Leah wiped a tear from her eye as she watched Larissa and Solomon dance for the first time as husband and wife. If God was merciful, He would bring someone in her life that would love her for a lifetime. A love of her own. Someone who only had eyes for her.

Chef Darnel had outdone himself on the beef, smashed potatoes and roasted asparagus. She headed into the kitchen to thank him and to take her mind off of how lonely she was at this moment. But the man's attitude had not changed one bit.

"No lookie-loos. How many times do I have to tell you not to bother me when I'm in the kitchen?"

"The food has already been served, Chef. I was just taking a moment to thank you because the meal was scrumptious."

"Of course, it was. I'm a professional. You don't have to come into the kitchen to thank me. Just make sure the check clears, that's plenty thanks for me."

That was it. She was thankful that the meal was so good, and all the guests were happy, but she wouldn't recommend Chef Darnel to cater anything ever again. Good riddance. She let her three-inch heels carry her out of the kitchen and then went to the cake table to get a glass of punch.

The bride and groom dance had ended and others were now headed to the floor with their dates. She walked toward the head table to sit down.

Before she could get there, a voice behind her asked, "Can I have this dance?"

Leah swung around, almost spilling her punch.

"I'm sorry. So sorry." Cory said. "I'm always scaring you. It's not intentional, I promise."

She shook her head. "You didn't scare me. I don't think I will ever forget the sound of your smooth, sexy voice."

"I don't want you to ever forget anything about me, Leah."

She smirked. "See how smooth you are?"

He held out a hand. "What about that dance?"

"Let me put my drink on the table." She put the punch down and took his hand. *I Found Love* by BeBe Winans was playing. He swung her onto the dance floor, pulled her close and held on tight. To take her mind off of the body heat his closeness was drawing she said, "I'm surprised you came."

"You did send me the invitation. I thought that meant it was okay for me to show my face." Staring down at her, looking into her eyes, he asked, "Am I wrong about that?"

"Oh, you're not wrong. I just didn't think you'd show. I thought you'd be working hard on your next big deal." She averted her gaze from his deep brown eyes. Eyes that seemed to read her every thought... *Lord, don't let him know what I'm thinking right now.*

"It would be hard for me to be at work when I don't have a job anymore."

The music hadn't stopped. But Leah couldn't move. Her hands fell from his shoulders. "What did you say?"

"You heard me."

"But why, I don't understand."

People around them were moving to the music but Leah and Cory stood staring at each other. Trying to figure out what this moment in time would mean for them.

"I prayed about everything you said to me, Leah." He put a finger under her chin and lifted her face so they were gazing into each others eyes. "And I want you to know that I don't want anything on this earth as much as I want you. I'm here for you, if you will have me."

"But...but...what are you going to do without a job?"

He tilted his head and gave a big belly laugh. When he stopped laughing, he told her, "I don't think I'll starve." Walking her off the dance floor, they sat at his table. "I'm working with some investors for a business of my own. I want to start a program for teens, something to help give them direction for their lives. Because I know all too well the things that can happen to take a kid who gets off course."

Grinning, Leah wrapped her arms around him. "Look at you," she said. "You should have gone to school for social work."

"You think you want to help me with some of this social work?"

Sitting down, Leah was speechless for a moment. Then she asked, "You really want me... working with you to help the youth?" Leah had dealt with so many self-esteem issues in her teen years. She was sure that many young girls were just like her. Maybe if she could reach out to girls who were just like her, and let them know that life does get better, she could help someone not inflict pain on their loved one, simply because they themselves were in pain.

"I need you, Leah. I don't want to do this work without you," Cory said.

"Yes, yes, I'd love to help." She was imagining all the good she could do for other young girls, when Solomon walked over to them.

Solomon held his cell phone in his hand and looked like something heavy was on his mind. And that seemed odd to Leah, since this was his wedding day.

"What going on?" she asked.

Solomon shook hands with Cory, slipping his phone in his pocket. "Hey man, thanks so much for coming out today."

"I wouldn't have missed it," Cory told him.

Solomon then turned back to Leah. "I just got off the phone with the prosecutor who has been handling Ned's case. I asked them to keep me posted on any new developments."

Leah put hands to her ears. "It's your wedding day, Solomon. I don't want to hear anything about that man. I don't want to hear his name at all."

Solomon held up a hand. "Sis, I'm sorry to tell you this, but I don't want you to hear it from anyone else... Ned was murdered in his jail cell last night."

For a moment, the world seemed to tilt. Leah knew she was supposed to feel some kind of way. Ned no longer had to exist in her head and she could just erase him. She should be jumping up and down with relief. But she just felt numb. "Thanks for telling me, Solomon.

Her words sounded flat, even to her, so she understood why Cory and Solomon were staring at her as if they were waiting on some type of explosion. "Stop staring at me, guys. I'm fine. He's dead and I no longer have to wonder when he will leave prison and come after me again. I'm good."

"Alright, Sis, but if you want to talk just hit me up when I get back from my honeymoon."

Leah playfully shoved Solomon towards Larissa. "If you don't get over there and stop worrying about me."

When Solomon left, Cory asked, "You sure you're okay?"

"Couldn't be better."

"Leah, you don't have to be strong for me. I'm here for you. I've got big broad shoulders for you to lean on."

She loved that he wanted to be here for her. Loved that he wanted to build the next phase of his life with her. Cory was the man of her dreams. He was the one her heart could love for a lifetime. She leaned forward, holding onto his tie and pulling him to her. Their lips touched and she finally felt the magic once again.

~ Chapter Twenty-Four

The choir was on point, performing to the glory of God under the direction of the new minister of music, Marla Williams. Marla, had told them the truth when they met her at that restaurant, she wasn't just a wonderful chef, the woman could sing like nobody's business.

She was turning out to be a great fit for the church. The words of the old hymn, "What a Friend We Have in Jesus" kept running through Leah's head long after the congregation had finished singing.

Leah smiled at Cory, seated next to her. Then she turned to her other side and addressed her mother. "This place is really jumping."

Her mother nodded, beaming. "I can almost see the Lord smiling as He sits on high, enthroned in the very praises drifting heavenward from here."

The thought of that made Leah smile too. It made her feel good to know that the Lord took delight in their praises. Even though she knew she would never be able to repay God for all He had done in her life, Leah wasn't going to stop trying.

After the praise and worship portion of the service, her father stepped behind the pulpit. He offered a quick word of prayer, then asked everyone to turn in their Bibles to the gospel of Matthew, chapter 18. He started reading from verse 21.

"'Then came Peter to him, and said, Lord, how oft shall my brother sin against me, and I forgive him? till seven times? Jesus saith unto him, I say not unto thee, Until seven times: but, Until seventy times seven. Therefore is the kingdom of heaven likened unto a certain king....'"

Leah had been feeling good, because the church service had been electrifying. But what her father had just read from the Bible had killed her mood. It was as if God was telling her to forgive Ned. But wasn't it too late, since he was dead?

Closing his Bible, her father looked out at the congregation. "When we gave our lives to the Lord, we asked Him to forgive us of all our sins. I can tell you that my sins were many. So, I was grateful beyond words when the Lord wiped my slate clean."

"Amen," shouted several dozen congregants.

"You know it."

"I was grateful too."

"But how many of us have decided that someone else has done too much harm to be forgiven?" her father went on. "Remember, forgiveness is not for the other person; it's for you. When you forgive, you free yourself so that you can move on with your life as a happy and whole individual, ready to love and to be loved. But if you can't forgive, you will never experience all that God has for you."

Leah knew he would say that. She respected her father and believed he was a true man of God, but there were some things Bishop David Davison didn't understand. He had never been beaten and stalked by a madman. He had never been tormented by thoughts of worthlessness.

Leah tried to sit there and soak up the message. She knew God was speaking to her, trying to get her to do what would be best for her Christian walk. Leah understood all of that, but she couldn't make her heart forgive. Not right now. Not when the pain Ned had inflicted was still so raw.

She stood, exited the pew, and made her way down the aisle toward the nearest women's restroom. She spent several minutes crying, giving God every excuse she could come up with for not forgiving Ned.

When she was done with her pity party, Leah dried her eyes, dabbed a little foundation on her face to cover up the tear streaks, and then returned to the service. Her father was wrapping up his message.

Cory put a hand over hers. "You alright?"

She nodded, not trusting her voice enough to speak her thoughts. Then Leah caught the look her mother was giving her. Her mother hadn't bought her need for a bathroom break in the middle of the sermon. Leah prayed that her mother would let it go. She wasn't ready to discuss her forgiveness issues.

Thankfully, by the time her father came down from the pulpit after the service, all her family members were so hungry that they just wanted to rush back to the house and fill their bellies. Leah's mother had made her famous turkey meat loaf with mac and cheese, sautéed greens, and candied yams. Her siblings added a leaf to the dining room table to make it large enough to accommodate two guests: Cory, of course, and their new minister of music, Marla Williams.

"Let's dig in," Adam said once the serving dishes were on the table.

"Hold on there," Leah's father said. "We need to offer grace over this wonderful food."

Adam put down the pan of meat loaf and Solomon returned the big spoon to the bowl of mac and cheese.

Then her father folded his hands and bowed his head. "Dear Lord, I can see that my boys are hungry, so I'm going to make this quick today. Please bless this food and the beautiful hands that prepared it."

"Amen," Adam said as he reached for the meat loaf again.

"Now, Father," Leah's dad continued. Adam retracted his hand. "This family is so grateful for all Your wondrous works. We're thankful, Father, and we will forever give You praise, even for mere food on the table. But, if it would not be too presumptuous, we would also like to thank You for life, health, and the strength to live our lives in a manner that glorifies You."

Several voices around the table shouted, "Amen!"

"Amen," Leah's father said with a chuckle. "*Now* we can eat. Somebody, please send the meatloaf and mac and cheese my way."

"You're not right, you know that, don't you?" Solomon teased as he passed the mac and cheese.

"Oh, you know I'm just messing with you and your brother. Y'all go on and fill your plates."

"I was going to get my meatloaf first, anyway," Adam told him. "If I wait until this plate gets back to me, with all y'all hungry folks, who knows if there would even be any left?"

Leah was happy to see that Adam was once again in a playful mood. He actually looked like he was enjoying himself, for the first time in months. She wondered if her brother had been able to forgive her for what she'd done to him. She couldn't blame him if he never did, but she hoped he would.

As she entertained that thought, she realized she was feeling exactly what her father had preached about that morning. She wanted forgiveness from Adam for all the havoc her wrongdoings had wreaked upon his life, but she refused to forgive Ned for the wrong he had done to her. *Oh, God, what am I going to do about that?*

Suddenly, she had to know whether her brother had forgiven her. He was seated next to her, so she leaned over and asked quietly, "Can I speak with you in the family room for a moment?"

Adam looked from his sister to his plate. "Can't this wait until after dinner? All I've eaten today is an apple."

"Please, Adam?" she persisted. "If you can wait a minute or two, I'd really like to speak with you now."

Adam winked and stood. "You better be glad you're my favorite sister."

"Hey," Tamara complained.

"You're my favorite sister, too, Tamara…and you too, Larissa," Adam said before following Leah from the room.

"After hearing Daddy's message this morning, I was convicted for refusing to forgive that monster Ned for what he did to me."

"Don't beat yourself up over that, Sis," Adam told her. "You went through a horrific experience. It takes time to heal from something like that."

Leah lifted her hand. "I'm not excusing myself. I wanted to talk to you because I believe what Daddy said about forgiveness—that it's for the benefit of the person who was wronged. It frees him or her to live healthy and whole, without bitterness. I don't want anything to hold you back from living your life, so I wanted to ask you to forgive me for the way I messed up your life. I am probably doomed to carry bitterness around with me for the rest of my life, but I don't want you to live that way because of any unforgiveness you might harbor toward me. I know how it feels to carry that load. It's heavy. Some days, it really weighs me down."

"Sis, I have already forgiven you. It wasn't your fault I had a child out of wedlock and kept her a secret. If I hadn't acted so foolishly, none of the things you blame yourself for would have ever happened."

"But—"

"No buts about it. I love Winter, and I'm thankful to have her in my life. That girl is going to make something of herself, and she has you to thank for that."

Leah hadn't thought of it that way. But the truth was, Winter's mother had been a complete mess. She wasn't fit to raise a pet, let alone a human being. But now, Summer was getting her life together, and Adam was able to be there for Winter. He had even set up a college fund for her. Without Adam, Winter wouldn't be able to think about college.

"Thanks for saying that, Adam."

"Sure. Now can I eat my food? Daddy is probably stealing all the meatloaf."

Giggling, Leah followed him back to the dining room.

When they had finished dinner, just before dessert was served, Cory stood up from his chair, got down on one knee, and asked Leah, "What are you doing for the next fifty years?"

She laughed. "I don't know. Why?"

He took a small box out of his jacket pocket. When he opened it, the brightness of the diamond ring shined throughout the room. "Because I want to marry you."

She shook her head. "If you can't promise me at least sixty years, it's a no-go."

"Lady, I can promise you an eternity." He kissed her, then said, "Make my dreams come true, Leah. God brought you back into my life because you and I were meant to be together. Forever."

She loved that his dream was no longer singularly about becoming richer than Bill Gates but that it now included her and their love. She could work with that.

"So, you're saying I'm the one for you?" Leah asked.

"Uh-uh, I'm saying, you're the only one for me."

"When you put it that way, how could I say no? Of course, I will marry you." She kissed him again. Thankful that God had sent the one, that was truly for her.

~Chapter Twenty-Five

Leah never imagined marrying the man of her dreams, but since it was happening, the event planner in her desired a destination wedding. They settled on the Bahamas in the summertime.

Cory had booked a block of rooms for the wedding party and their guests at the Grand Lucayan. Leah loved everything about the place. The moment they arrived, a feeling of serenity washed over her like a gentle wave, washing away all the worries of the world.

Their wedding ceremony would take place on the beach. A tent had been set up with tables and chairs for the reception. Marla had come to the Bahamas to cater their meal and sing a solo. Leah should have felt brand new but something gnawed at her.

Marla was the first to notice Leah's wariness. The two women had become close friends over the past several months. "What's wrong, Leah?" Marla asked, seated at the piano in the sanctuary. She'd been practicing the song Leah had requested she perform at the ceremony. "You look like you're ready to bolt."

"I do not," Leah insisted.

Marla stood and walked over to her. "Yeah, you do. Was coming to the Bahamas too much for you? I'm sure your family will understand if you tell them that you'd rather go back home to get married."

"It's not that," Leah said. She was about to say more, but then her parents walked in with Cory not far behind them.

"There you are." Cory came up to her and gave her a kiss. "You took off so fast, I didn't know if you had gone into the church or if you were walking down the beach."

"I wanted to get inside the church so I could see the beautiful decorations before the rehearsal," she told him.

Cory looked around the sanctuary. "It's beautiful, babe." It was decorated with their wedding theme of silver and fig, which, Leah had explained to Cory, was a cross between purple and fuchsia.

"Do you really think so?" Leah asked, then frowned. "I'm not so sure. I might have made a mistake on the colors."

"Are you kidding?" her mother said as she and Leah's father walked up to them. "This place looks wonderful. I wouldn't change a thing."

Breathe... breathe. Everything is fine, Leah tried to calm her nerves. But her self-talk wasn't working.

Leah turned to her father. "What about you, Daddy? Do you think I made a mistake coming all the way to the Bahamas to get married? I mean, you have that great big church back home in Charlotte, and yet we traveled all this way for a simple ceremony. That's crazy, right?" Leah started laughing, and before long, she was in hysterics.

Everyone watched her nervously, but she found she couldn't stop.

"Is she having a panic attack?" Marla asked the group.

Cory grabbed hold of Leah and started for the door. "Can you all make sure everything is taken care of here?" he asked over his shoulder. "I need to talk to my bride."

"We'll take care of everything," Leah's mother assured him. "Don't worry about a thing in here. Just calm her down."

Once they were outside, walking down the beach, Cory said, "Please, honey, tell me what's gotten you?"

Leah took a few deep breaths, finally calming down. "What makes you think anything's wrong?"

Cory stopped walking, lifted her hands to his lips, and kissed her fingertips, one at a time. "Because I know you, sweetheart. You haven't been yourself since we arrived in the Bahamas."

"It's not what you think," Leah said to reassure her man. "I'm not nervous about marrying you. I love you and want to be your wife more than anything else in the world."

"Then what is it?"

When she didn't answer, Cory ran the back of his hand down the side of her face. "The only way we're going to have a successful marriage is if we start our life together the right way."

Closing her eyes, she put her hand to her heart. "I don't want to lose you."

"Don't shut me out, babe. I'm right here, and I'm not going anywhere, no matter what the problem is."

"But that's just it." Leah's eyes filled with unshed tears. "You won't be here for me if I don't fix this. My hard heart will eventually drive you away."

He frowned. "What are you talking about? You don't have a hard heart. You're the gentlest, most loving person I know."

She turned from Cory, not wanting to see his face as she broke his heart. "I can't do it. Maybe I'm not the right woman for you. We need to call off the wedding."

Cory reached for her and tried to draw her toward him. "I'm not calling off our wedding, Leah. What's this all about?"

Pulling away, she said, "Just let it be, Cory."

"We have to get back for the rehearsal, Leah. Come on, this doesn't make any sense."

Backing away from him. "I need a little time to myself." She took off running down the beach.

~~~

Cory wanted to chase after Leah and beg her to think about what she was doing and how her actions would affect them for the rest of their lives. But she'd asked him to give her time and he would.

Adam parked the car at the church and came over to Cory. "Was that Leah I saw running?"

Cory's shoulders slumped. "She said she needs time to think."

"Think about what? Did your stock just plummet and she's trying to figure out if she wants to live in poverty with you?"

"No, my stock didn't plummet. I don't think jokes are appropriate at a time like this."

Adam put an arm around Cory's shoulders. "You're right. I'm sorry for cracking jokes. Leah loves you. She won't go far. Don't worry. She'll be back."

They went inside the church and joined the others who had gathered for the rehearsal. When they joined the group, Alma's eyes flickered with questions.

"Where's Leah?" Bishop Davison asked.

"She's out on the beach, taking some time for herself," Cory said, unable to keep his misery out of his tone.

"I could tell something was bothering her," Marla said as she stepped away from the piano.

"Cold feet," Alma said. "That's all it is. She'll be back in a minute, I'm sure."

Cory shook his head. "She doesn't have cold feet. She told me that she wants to marry me more than anything. But she's worried that—these are her words, now—her 'hard heart' will ruin our marriage."

"What hard heart?" Tamara asked as she joined the group. "And where is Leah?"

"Leah is off on her own, trying to figure out what she wants," Cory said. "She thinks she has a hard heart, and I don't know what she's talking about." He sighed. "I told her that I don't know anybody who's gentler or more loving than she is, but she refuses to believe it. She has shut me out." He sat down in the front pew and hung his head.

Just then, Larissa and Solomon entered the tent.

"I thought we were supposed to be rehearsing for a wedding," Solomon said. "Where's the bride?"

"She needed space," Alma told him. "In the meantime, we can go on and rehearse without her."

"How are we going to rehearse without the bride?" Cory asked, getting up from his seat. "Doesn't she need to see how everything is going to go? Approve of all the details?"

Alma walked over to him and put a hand on his shoulder. "Do you still want to marry Leah?"

Cory nodded. "More than anything."

"Then listen to what I'm telling you. The bride doesn't need to know anything that's going on before she starts her procession up the aisle. So, let's all work on that, get it perfected for her, and then David will guide Leah right to you tomorrow. Okay?"

Cory couldn't help but be skeptical.

Then David stepped forward. "I agree with Alma that we should rehearse without Leah. But before we do that, we need to pray.

Something has driven her away from here, and if we all come together in prayer, I am confident that God will bring about a change with Leah."

"She definitely doesn't have a hard heart," Cory remarked. He wasn't going to let anyone think badly of his bride, even if she thought badly of herself.

"I agree with you," David told Cory. "But she says she does, and we must take her at her word." He looked around at the others. "Now, I'm getting ready to pray. Won't you all join me?"

Adam raised his hand like a student in grade school.

"What is it, Son?"

"I've been standing here, mulling this over, and I think I know what's eating at Leah." He moved closer to the rest of his family, now gathered around the altar. "A few months ago"—he pointed at Cory—"the same day you proposed to Leah, Dad preached a message about forgiveness. That afternoon, Leah asked me to forgive her for bringing confusion into my life. But I told her that I had already forgiven her.

"Anyway, she said the reason she was asking for forgiveness was because she wanted me to be able to live a life free of bitterness. She also said she still hadn't been able to forgive Ned, and that she would probably carry bitterness toward him for the rest of her life."

"I didn't know she was still thinking about that monster," Cory admitted. "I told her to come to me if she needed to talk about him."

"I think we know what to pray for," David said. He held his hands, and the family linked together in a circle as they took Leah's problem to the throne of grace.

~~~

The captain of the host had been summoned. He didn't waste time wondering why; he just left his host of angels and made his way to the Holy Place. He opened the massive doors laden with gold and stood in the rear. The voice of thunder and lightning was speaking, so there was no one milling about. No one entered or departed this Most Holy Place unless commanded to do so. As the Lord sat on His throne, a multitude of praises went up: "Holy, holy, holy." And as the voices became thunderous, Aaron bowed down, joining in the praise. In this place, where God sits high and is lifted up, praises are sung to Him forever. His glory and love filled the atmosphere, and joy spread throughout His heavenly court.

Thunder and lightning sparkled from the throne of grace, and then Michael stood. His colorful wings glistened as they flapped. "Yes, my Lord," he said, taking the scrolls from the Omnipotent hand which held them.

Jewels were embedded throughout the handle of Michael's massive sword, symbolizing his many victories. And the belt where his sword was holstered sparkled with the gold of heaven.

Michael held out the scrolls to Aaron. "Here is your assignment."

Aaron took them. "Thank you for entrusting this mission to us," he told him. "We will get it done."

~Chapter Twenty-Six

Leah was despondent as she shuffled down the beach. The water was clear and blue; the warm sun beat down upon her face. Lovers strolled the beach, holding hands, while she cried her eyes out. Loving Cory as much as she did, Leah couldn't bear the thought that her own deep-rooted bitterness might someday be the thing that would bring about division in their home.

Leah was at a loss for how to make what she felt go away. She didn't mourn the Ned's death, but some nights, she had nightmares about the events that had occurred in her DC hotel suite. Specifically, when Ned was being carted out of her room by the police, she had wished him being killed in prison.

The man of her dreams was waiting for her, wondering what was wrong with her, wondering why she wanted to call off their wedding. The way she saw it, if she couldn't bring herself to walk down that aisle tomorrow and marry Cory, then Ned was to blame. Why should she forgive him for ruining her life?

An invisible barrier stopped her in her tracks. It felt as if she'd collided with a force field. When she looked up, she saw a tall man. "Excuse me," she said. "I didn't see you there."

"You are to blame. No one else," he said before walking away.

"Geeze." Leah frowned and resumed walking. What had gotten that man so upset? And what did he mean by saying she was to blame, and no one else? Hadn't she apologized for bumping into him?

As she continued to walk, Leah noticed that she'd somehow returned to the hotel. She didn't understand; she had taken off walking in the opposite direction. Yet, here she was, standing in the same spot she and Cory had stood when she had ran off.

The man she'd seen was now headed in her direction. Fear gripped her heart. She worried that he might attack her or retaliate in some other way. Her mind said *Run*, but her feet remained planted in the sand.

When he reached her, he said once again, "You are to blame."

"I already apologized, mister," she told him. "But, in case you didn't hear me the first time, I'm sorry. I didn't mean to bump you like that."

"What if I don't accept your apology?" the man asked.

"Well, you should." That was all Leah could come up with. She didn't understand what the big deal was.

"Why? Because you want my forgiveness, even though you deny forgiveness to others?"

Stepping back as fear jumped into her heart, she said, "Who are you? What do you want?"

"Your family is praying, but it's time for you to do your part, Leah. Put the blame where it belongs," he said.

Was this man saying she was at fault for the terrible things that had happened in her life? Leah wrapped her arms around her chest and turned away. Who was he to speak to her that way? He didn't know anything about her or her situation. She turned back to tell him just that, but he was gone.

Rubbing her chin as she realized that he hadn't meant she was to blame for what had happened to her, but rather for her reaction to it. The bitterness she had allowed to take root in her heart, existed because she'd refused to forgive and move forward with her life.

Leah slumped to the ground, her tears blending with the sand and made a puddle. She opened her mouth and began to pray.

"Lord, I need You. I rededicated my life to You but I have been keeping a part of myself from You—the part that I reserved the right to hate Ned Turner. Even though I know Your Word says that a double-minded man is unstable in all his ways, I still claimed to love You while hating someone else.

But this hate, this bitterness—it's destroying me. It's taking from me the man I love. The man I desire to spend the rest of my life with. This isn't fair to him, and it isn't fair to me. Ned is dead and gone, so I need You to fix my heart. Take away the pain that is causing me so much bitterness.

"What he did was wrong, but what I'm doing to the ones I love —harboring bitterness against someone else, and consequently making Cory pay for another man's crime—is even worse. I don't want to be like this. Because I know that if I don't let this go, I will not hurt Cory and bring additional harm to my family. Bitterness is my natural inclination," she confessed, thinking of the way she'd treated Larissa while growing up. "But You can make me better. So, I'm calling on You, Lord Jesus, to change me, so that I will not wreak havoc in the lives of the ones I love. Make me new, Lord Jesus, and I will forever give You the praise. Amen."

~~~

"Well, that's it," Alma declared. "We've prayed and we've practiced. I think we're ready for tomorrow."

"All we have to do now is find Leah and head to the rehearsal dinner," Cory said glumly.

Joining in prayer with his new family had reignited his faith that Leah would come to her senses. That everything would turn out alright. But they had been at the church for hours, and she hadn't returned.

"Why don't we each take a section of the beach and search for her?" David suggested. "She probably purchased a book and is stretched out somewhere reading, trying to calm her mind."

"No, I'm not, Daddy."

Cory pivoted toward the direction of Leah's voice.

"I've been on the beach, praying for the strength to forgive Ned." She stood in the doorway, looking as if she'd been in the middle of a whirlwind. Her eyes were bloodshot, and her foundation had been washed away with the tears that had streaked down her face.

To Cory, she was a beautiful sight. He rushed over to her and wrapped her in his arms. "I'm so glad you came back. I was so worried."

"I was, too," she admitted. "But for different reasons." She held Cory's hands. "I never want to be a burden or a curse to you."

"And you never will be," he assured her.

"Let me finish." She hugged him again. "My hatred for Ned was beginning to drown out the love I have for you. I couldn't marry you as long as my hate for someone was greater than my love for you."

Cory held her at arm's length and looked into her eyes. "I had no idea you felt that way." Now he was the one having second thoughts. Maybe Leah was right—maybe it wasn't time for them to get married. He didn't think their marriage would survive if her hatred of another man outweighed her love for him.

"But as I walked the beach," she continued, "God was with me. I felt the power of God come strongly over me as I prayed and prayed to be able to forgive that man. And, finally, I was able to release him."

A wave of relief and gratitude to God washed over Cory as Leah stepped away from him and approached Bishop Davison.

"Daddy, your message about forgiveness was so true. The moment I forgave Ned for all the horrible things he did to me… it was at that moment that I felt free to love."

The entire family started to praise God for her deliverance. Leah walked back over to Cory and told him, "I'm sorry for what I said earlier. I don't want to cancel our wedding. Will you please marry me and give me a reason to believe in happy endings?"

He grinned. "I planned to be right here wearing my tux first thing in the morning. We've already rehearsed, so we're all prepared."

Leah frowned. "Y'all practiced without me?"

"You ran off, we had no choice," Larissa told her with a grin.

"But…I need to know what's going to go on at my own wedding. Can we just run through everything again?"

"No!" the group shouted.

"We're starving," Adam informed her. "You are not about to deprive us of our long-awaited and well-deserved rehearsal dinner."

Leah looked at Cory. "And you're okay with this?"

"Babe, dinner was planned for six. We need to get back to the hotel and change."

"But…" Leah tried again.

"Everything will be fine. All you have to do is come down that aisle and say 'I do.' Trust us. God gave you the victory over Ned, once and for all. And, we had your back. Our wedding is going to be beautiful."

Leah looked thoughtful for a moment. "You're right," she acquiesced. "I'm not going to worry about how the wedding is going to turn out, because I'm in this for the marriage, and I now know that our marriage will be as wonderful as we make it."

~~~

A catered meal awaited the group at the hotel. Once they had changed into their evening attire—floor-length gowns for the women, black suits and ties for the men—they were ready to get the party started. And no one was more ready than Leah and Cory.

This was their happy every after, a dream come true and they were walking into it with all the love they had to give… and that was enough.

~ Chapter Twenty-Seven

Leah couldn't stop studying her reflection in the full-length mirror that leaned against the wall of the church bathroom. The church was steps away from the beach. The pastor had been kind enough to allow them to use the church to get dressed.

Her floor-length cream-colored wedding gown made her look more elegant than the Duchess of Cambridge on her wedding day. The way Cory treated her, she felt as if she were marrying her Prince Charming.

Her mother walked into the room, saw her, and burst into tears. "You look so beautiful." She took Leah's arm and twirled her around. "You are always stylish, but this gown is elegant."

Hugging her mother, Leah said, "Thank you for saying that. The funny thing is, I never believed you when you said things like that before. But I believe it today. Letting go of all that bitterness I had been carrying around has helped to open my eyes. I now see myself as God sees me."

"I'm so happy for you, honey."

"And I'm so happy to be marrying Cory. God couldn't have picked a better mate for me."

Her mother chuckled. "So glad you approve of God's choice. Your dad and I can't wait to welcome Cory into the family."

"Thank you, Mama. Are you sure Dad isn't upset that I didn't get married at the church?"

"No hon, we know how much you love the thrill of planning events. And we are fine with this."

"Good, because I can't wait for daddy to walk me down the aisle. I have the best parents in the world and I'm so grateful for you."

"We love you, Leah." Then with a bit of mischievousness in her eyes, she added, "and I'm grateful for the excuse to get your dad to take another vacation."

"Thanks for being so understanding, Mom. I always wanted a destination wedding, and I feel at peace in this place."

"Then it's settled. Now, let's go get you married off."

~~~

Cory watched the flower girl—his little cousin—saunter down the aisle, tossing a handful of rose petals with every step she took. His gaze swept over his groomsmen—Leah's brothers—standing with him, and then Leah's bridesmaids, all standing with bouquets in hand.

As the bridal processional song began to play, Cory looked down the aisle and caught the loveliest vision in white that he'd ever seen. Leah's dress was silky and flowed all the way to the floor. She held on to her father's arm as she strode down the aisle, looking nervous and excited at the same time.

Cory found himself thinking back to the days when they were in youth group and high school together. From the first time he'd seen Leah, he'd known that she was the one. It had taken Leah a lot longer to figure that out. The path back to each other had been a rough one, but they had made it, and now, nothing would ever separate them again.

When Leah's father handed her off to Cory, he took her hand and pulled her close. Her father took his place in front of them and then cleared his throat. He then opened his Bible and read a passage from the book of Genesis, followed by Proverbs 18:22: *"Whoso findeth a wife findeth a good thing, and obtaineth favour of the LORD."*

Her father went on to encourage them about the benefits of marriage. Then he addressed the guests and asked, "Is there anyone here who knows of a reason these two should not be joined together?"

No one spoke out against Leah or Cory, so her father returned his attention to Cory and said, "Repeat after me."

Cory held Leah's hand, looked her in the eyes, and waited for the opportunity to repeat his vows.

Following Bishop Davison's lead, Cory said, "I, Cory Parker, take you, Leah Davison, to be my wedded wife." After that first statement, Cory felt as if his heart was about to explode with all the love he possessed for Leah.

He felt calmer as he continued repeating after Bishop Davison.

"Now, here's the really important part," Bishop Davison said as he led Cory in a pledge of faithfulness to Leah.

Cory repeated the words, Leah's eyes became moist. He wanted to wrap her in his arms and wipe each tear away.

Bishop Davison then turned to Leah and said, "Repeat these words after me: I, Leah Davison, take you, Cory Parker, to be my wedded husband."

"I, Leah Davison, take you, Cory Parker, to be my wedded husband…"

Once the rest of her vows had been spoken, Bishop Davison told Cory to kiss his bride. Cory didn't need any more encouragement. He pulled Leah to him and went in like a man who'd been in the desert dying of thirst. "That settles it," he told her as they came up for air. "You are mine forever now."

"I wouldn't have it any other way." Putting a hand on Cory's cheek she said, "I found my dream and I am never ever going to let you go.

The end.

Once Upon A Dream

Book 2 in the Dreaming of Love

Series

releases on June 15, 2021

Book Discussion Questions

1) Leah's character comes from the Biblical story of Leah, who was always second best in Jacob's eyes. The Leah of this story felt as if she was second, and sometimes even third best. Do you think that played a part in her lack of self worth or was it just all of her own making? Why?

2) Why do you think Leah had such a hard time understanding why Winter and the rest of her family loved on her in her time of need? Have you ever had a problem accepting kindness from others? Why?

3) Cory feels that saving Leah from Ned Turner is a kind of atonement for not being able to help his cousin. But do you think Cory was carrying around guilt that wasn't his to bear?

4) Where do you think Leah's tendency to be vindictive came from? When Leah returned to work and was about to plot revenge against Donna, but then stopped and prayed, did you see growth in her or did she still seem vindictive? Have you ever been vindictive in your life, and then later wished you had made a different decision?

5)   What about Donna Phillips, do you think she was truly sorry for the way she went about getting her promotion? Should Leah have forgiven her? Why or why not?

6)   Leah and her mother loved each other, but they had a complicated relationship. What or who do you think caused their issues?

~Fear Not Scriptures

Dear Reader, these have been some scary times lately, but when you are afraid, I pray that you find comfort in the Word of God. He will never leave you, nor forsake you.

Psalm 27:1
"The Lord is my light and my salvation—whom shall I fear? The Lord is the stronghold of my life—of whom shall I be afraid?" Used Already

Psalm 55:22
"Cast your cares on the Lord and he will sustain you; he will never let the righteous fall." Used Already

Deuteronomy 31:6
"Be strong and courageous. Do not be afraid or terrified because of them, for the Lord your God goes with you; he will never leave you nor forsake you." Used Already

Isaiah 41:13-14

"'For I am the Lord, your God, who takes hold of your right hand and says to you, Do not fear; I will help you. Do not be afraid, for I myself will help you,' declares the Lord, your Redeemer, the Holy One of Israel." Used Already

Psalm 46:1
"God is our refuge and strength, an ever-present help in trouble."

Psalm 118:6-7
"The Lord is with me; I will not be afraid. What can man do to me? The Lord is with me; he is my helper." Used Already

Proverbs 29:25
"Fear of man will prove to be a snare, but whoever trusts in the Lord is kept safe." used already

Mark 4:39-40
"He got up, rebuked the wind and said to the waves, "Quiet! Be still!" Then the wind died down and it was completely calm. He said to his disciples, "Why are you so afraid? Do you still have no faith?"

Psalm 34:7
"The angel of the Lord encamps around those who fear him, and he delivers them."

1 Peter 3:14
"But even if you suffer for doing what is right, God will reward you for it. So don't worry or be afraid of their threats."

Psalm 34:4

"I prayed to the Lord, and he answered me. He freed me from all my fears."

Isaiah 41:10
"So do not fear, for I am with you; do not be dismayed, for I am your God. I will strengthen you and help you; I will uphold you with my righteous right hand."

Psalm 56:3
"When I am afraid, I put my trust in you."

Don't forget to join my mailing list:
http://vanessamiller.com/events-join-mailing-list/

Join me on Facebook: https://www.facebook.com/Author-Vanessa-Miller-106334304622871/?ref=pages_you_manage
Join me on Twitter: https://www.twitter.com/vanessamiller01
Join me on Instagram: https://www.instagram.com/authorvanessamiller

Other Books by Vanessa Miller

Something Good (rel. March 2022)
Dream Come True

Once Upon A Dream

Forever

Family Business I

Family Business II

Family Business III

Family Business IV

Family Business V

Family Business VI

Our Love

For Your Love

Got To Be Love

Rain in the Promised Land

Sunshine And Rain

After the Rain

How Sweet The Sound

Heirs of Rebellion

Feels Like Heaven

The Best of All

Better for Us

Her Good Thing

Long Time Coming

A Promise of Forever Love

A Love for Tomorrow

Yesterday's Promise

Forgotten

Forgiven

Forsaken

Rain for Christmas (Novella)

Through the Storm

Rain Storm

Latter Rain

Abundant Rain

Former Rain

Anthologies (Editor)

Keeping the Faith

Have A Little Faith

This Far by Faith

Novella

Love Isn't Enough

A Mighty Love

The Blessed One (Blessed and Highly Favored series)

The Wild One (Blessed and Highly Favored Series)

The Preacher's Choice (Blessed and Highly Favored Series)

The Politician's Wife (Blessed and Highly Favored Series)

The Playboy's Redemption (Blessed and Highly Favored Series)

Tears Fall at Night (Praise Him Anyhow Series)

Joy Comes in the Morning (Praise Him Anyhow Series)

A Forever Kind of Love (Praise Him Anyhow Series)

Ramsey's Praise (Praise Him Anyhow Series)

Escape to Love (Praise Him Anyhow Series)

Praise For Christmas (Praise Him Anyhow Series)

His Love Walk (Praise Him Anyhow Series)

Could This Be Love (Praise Him Anyhow Series)

Song of Praise (Praise Him Anyhow Series)

Excerpt of

Once Upon A Dream

Book 2

Dreaming of Love Series

Prologue

One by one, everyone took a seat and sat forward, looking attentive. Tamara's father, Bishop David Davison, opened his Bible and said, "Please turn with me to Psalm fifty-one." When the pages stopped turning, he began reading, starting with the first verse:

"Have mercy upon me, O God, according to thy lovingkindness: according unto the multitude of thy tender mercies blot out my transgressions. Wash me thoroughly from mine iniquity, and cleanse me from my sin. For I acknowledge my transgressions: and my sin is ever before me. Against thee, thee only, have I sinned, and done this evil in thy sight: that thou mightest be justified when thou speakest, and be clear when thou judgest. Behold, I was shapen in iniquity, and in sin did my mother conceive me. Behold, thou desirest truth in the inward parts: and in the hidden part thou shalt make me to know wisdom. Purge me with hyssop, and I shall be clean: wash me, and I shall be whiter than snow. Make me to hear joy and gladness; that the bones which thou hast broken may rejoice."

When he had finished reading, her father looked out over the congregation. Tears were running down his face as he said, "For months now, you all have heard false allegations against me, and those of you who love and know me believed us when we told you that what was being said about me wasn't true. I thank you for standing with us.

215

"But today, I stand before you and confess that I have sinned against my family and against God. For although those allegations were false, my wife and I have hidden another secret for thirty years. It wasn't right for us to do this, and it ends today."

Sitting next to her, Solomon was holding his breath, as if he could hardly believe what his ears were hearing. On his other side was, Larissa, who was her mother's niece but had been adopted by Tamara's parents when she was a child. So they were sisters. Larissa was now dating Solomon, which in Tamara's mind, was a bit awkward.

"You see," Tamara's father continued, "I am not a perfect man, just a man who happens to love Jesus. But before my wife and I gave our lives to the Lord, I had an affair with another woman, resulting in the birth of a son. My wife and I were separated at the time; but, as I counsel married couples all the time, separation doesn't give you the right to go out and hook up with someone other than your spouse. I learned the hard way that what I did was wrong, and my family has been paying for my infidelity ever since. The biggest price has been paid by my son Solomon, with whom I never had a relationship because I was too ashamed to acknowledge the sinful act I had committed."

He looked down at Solomon and said, "I hope that, one day, you will be able to forgive me for what I did, Son. Because I want to be your father more than anything in this world."

Tamara saw tears spring to Solomon's eyes when her father called him "Son." Then Solomon stood and strode over to the podium. He'd put his arms around her father and cried on his shoulder. "I forgive you, Dad," he sobbed. "I forgive you."

It had been a touching moment. Tamara had even shed a few tears. But it hadn't been long afterward when tongues had started wagging. Tamara was growing to love her half-brother but being a part of the Davison clan was too much drama.

Her close-knit family had always been known as a morally upright bunch, as pillars of the community. Tamara had been proud to be part of this family. But after what her father, Adam and Leah did… she wanted no part of them anymore. In truth, she just wanted to run and hide. So, she'd did the next best thing: quit her job at her father's church and accepted a position in Atlanta, almost four hours away from her family and the craziness that now surrounded them.

She prayed the craziness would not follow her there.

Two years later

Chapter 1

Snapping her fingers to Marvin Gaye's "Trouble Man," Tamara Davison tried to put herself in the right frame of mind for the interview she was scheduled to do the following day with the illustrious Jonathan Hartman. The man had indeed come up hard, as the words of the song repeated over and over; but there was nothing hard about Jonathan's life these days. It made Tamara wonder if this song was still on his playlist. Uncovering the answer to that question could be the start of an awesome interview series that could lead to a gig on CNN, or so she hoped.

Tamara was tired of the knockoff, wannabe, so-called travel station she was working for. She wanted more—much more. So far, she had been allowed in front of the camera only a few times since being hired by the network. Most of her time was spent writing copy for the lifestyle magazine the network owned.

She needed to make a move quickly, because she couldn't let things continue the way they had been going. If only she no longer depended on the monthly checks her father sent to her, as if money could cover his guilt for having ruined her life and destroying her ability to trust men in general. Only recently had she learned the truth about the father she had long considered perfect—a man who pastored a thriving megachurch in Charlotte. Years ago, he had fathered a child out of wedlock and kept it a secret for decades. And after he'd finally welcomed his illegitimate son back into the family fold, it had gotten out that Tamara's brother, Adam, had done the same thing as his old man. She was through with both of them, and with every other member of their species.

If this interview went well, she could start earning her own living and tell her father that he could keep his money.

***

Looking as dapper as ever in a khaki two-button blazer, snug fitted jeans, and dark brown slip-on Prada loafers, Jonathan Hartman was all smiles as he strutted into the banquet hall where this year's All About the Future luncheon was being held. This was Jonathan's third year hosting the event, at which he gave away college scholarships to deserving high school students. But this was his first time hosting in the town where he'd grown up, in New Orleans, Louisiana. And it was the first time in years that he'd been back. Fifteen years ago, he'd left home to attend the University of North Carolina–Chapel Hill. Shortly into his junior year, he'd transferred to Howard University in D.C. After graduating, he'd taken on his first fixer-upper, and he hadn't bothered looking back. He doubted anyone would blame him.

Jonathan vividly remembered the warm summer day when he'd glanced out the window and had seen the children playing in the front yard of the run-down house across the street. He'd wanted to join them, but after countless instances of begging his mother to let him, she'd finally given him an answer.

"You can't ever play with those kids," she'd told him flatly. "Your dad wouldn't like it, and then he would stop making his child-support payments."

"Where is my dad?" Jonathan remembered asking. "Why doesn't he ever come to see me?"

His mother had opened the curtain and pointed at the very house where those kids were playing. "Your dad lives there," she'd said.

"He's those kids' dad, too, and he don't want his precious wife knowing that he fathered a kid by another woman. Now do you understand why you can't go play with them?"

The news had shaken his seven-year-old world like nothing else. So deep was the wound that his mother's revelation had inflicted on him that he'd never been able to completely heal from the pain.

When tears had started rolling down his face that day, his mother had taken him in her arms. As she'd rocked him, she'd said, "I'm sorry, Son, but I guess it's high time you knew the truth. I wish I could take back what I did to you, but if I could, you wouldn't be here. We'll both just have to live with it."

After the hurt Jonathan experienced as a child, he'd never wanted to come back to this city. He felt no nostalgia for the Big Easy. Had no desire to walk through the French Quarter or sample the seafood, nor did he want to listen to any of the numerous jazz musicians posted on the street corners. Plus, his mother lived in Florida now, so it wasn't as if he'd been obligated to come back to visit her. But his business manager had informed him that they had received a petition signed by kids at three local high schools there, and Jonathan had finally agreed that he couldn't avoid this town any longer. But he'd made sure that the ballroom in which the luncheon was scheduled was on the opposite side of town from where he'd grown up.

"Mr. Hartman, thank God you're here!" his assistant, Lisa, greeted him. "You had me worried for a minute there."

Her worry was understandable—Jonathan was known for being early without fail for everything. His grandmother had been nicknamed "Early Bird" because she didn't just believe in being on time; she arrived well beforehand for everything. "The early bird gets the worm," she used to tell him. Jonathan had adopted the same behavior, and he'd gotten quite a few worms because of his grandmother's advice.

But Jonathan had delayed on purpose because he didn't plan on spending even one minute more than he had to in this town. "Everything's all set, then?

Lisa nodded. "Of course. I was just waiting on you to arrive so we could get started."

"Well, I'm here, so let's get things moving. I have a plane to catch."

She raised an eyebrow. "I thought you might want to hang around your hometown for a little while. Don't you have any old friends you want to see before heading back home?"

"Any friends I had here moved away a long time ago, just as I did." That was the easy response, much better than admitting that he hadn't made any lasting friends in this town. Jonathan had never felt good enough for anything or anyone until he went to college. But he hadn't kept many friends from college, either. Maybe he should change his bio, removing any reference to his birthplace. That way, no one would assume that he had any connections to this godforsaken town.

"Well, don't run off too fast, because you have an interview with Tamara Davison from the Word in Action network right after the luncheon."

He couldn't hide the smile that crept across his face—the first genuine grin he'd given since arriving here. "I won't forget. I'm looking forward to it."

Looking down at her notes, Lisa added, "Ms. Davison told me that the two of you are old acquaintances. Sounds like at least one of your former associates stuck around."

"Tamara isn't from here. I met her in college." Jonathan wanted to tell her that he and Tamara were friends, but the way things ended between them left a big question mark on that.

As Lisa jotted something on her notepad, Jonathan walked past her and entered the banquet hall. He was caught off guard as the room exploded with applause, all the banquet attendees standing to their feet. It wasn't that this was unusual for All About the Future events—he knew that Lisa always told the award recipients to applaud as soon as he entered the room. But, in this town, where he hadn't even been allowed to speak to his own father or play with the neighbor kids, the applause didn't seem warranted. It felt as if, at any moment, everyone would figure out who he was and revoke their applause, reminding him of the nobody he used to be.

"Thank you so much for what you're doing for our kids," one of the mothers said as she approached him with outstretched hand. "My son had given up on the idea of going to college until we found out about the scholarships your organization provides for underprivileged students."

"You don't have to thank me," Jonathan said as he shook her hand. "I'm just making good on a promise I made to God back when I didn't know how I would be able to afford college. The Lord made that happen for me…and so much more."

The woman beamed. "And it's my prayer that the Lord will do the same for my son, and for the rest of these kids, as well."

"Just tell him to dream big and stay focused, and I guarantee you, he will succeed."

The woman's eyes filled with tears as she put her hand on Jonathan's shoulder. "God bless you, Mr. Hartman. You are truly God-sent."

"I don't know about that, but I thank you for saying so."

Soon Jonathan took his place at the table where Tamara Davison was already seated. He smiled at her, praying that she wouldn't be able to tell what he was thinking. When they were in college together, Jonathan had dreamed about Tamara being his girl, but he'd never summoned the courage to ask her out. A cheerleader, she'd dated jocks exclusively, and Jonathan had always felt that he didn't measure up. In those days, that feeling had prevailed in just about every area of his life. So, he'd kept quiet about his attraction and contented himself with just being friends.

Finally, it had reached the point where Jonathan couldn't pretend any longer. That was when everything had changed.

But they weren't in college anymore. And Tamara had traveled a great distance to interview him. Maybe these days, being successful in business rather than on the basketball court or the football field meant something to her. He was about to lean across the table to say something to her, but the emcee took his place at the podium and began his opening remarks before he could do so.

Before long, Jonathan was summoned to the stage to award the scholarship certificates. There were twenty recipients in all. Ten of them would receive a full ride for four years, five of them would enjoy a full ride for two years, and the last five would have their first year of school covered. The extent of their reward was based on three simple areas: academic performance, community service, and financial need. Jonathan had established the criteria for the scholarships, but he never got involved in deciding who would receive them.

Once the emcee handed him the certificates, he stepped up to the podium and began calling the names of the recipients of the four-year full-ride scholarships. One by one, the awardees walked onstage, accompanied by their parents or guardians, to accept their certificates and shake his hand. They wore the grins of kids who knew that life would never be the same for them.

Handing out the certificates brought tears to Jonathan's eyes This ceremony was always bittersweet for him, because it brought back memories of how tough it had been to grow up in a single-parent household, raised by a mom who often didn't have enough money to put food on the table.

In those days, Jonathan had never imagined that he would make something of himself. He had certainly never thought he would enjoy the kinds of riches God had blessed him with. And that was the primary reason he gave back through the scholarship program Didn't the Bible say that it was more blessed to give than to receive? Jonathan appreciated all the people who had helped him along the way. He only prayed that these kids would someday come to experience the blessings of giving because of what had been given to them.

Finally, it was time for the third group of recipients to come up to the stage—those who would receive a one-year full-ride scholarship. Most of the students in this group had earned mediocre grades and had done just enough community service to get by. So, they were receiving awards compensatory to their labor. But each year, someone in this third tier always managed to do something that surprised Jonathan. When that happened, he made sure that the scholarship money kept flowing until he or she graduated. He wondered who would be the surprise in this year's group.

When he reached the second to last name, he stammered. "C-carter Washington." Reeling from the thoughts running through his head, Jonathan tried to calm himself. There had to be more than one Carter Washington in the state of Louisiana.

He recalled the last time he'd seen Carter, the only kid from across the street who'd ever said a word to him. He'd been two years old; Jonathan, fourteen. He remembered the moment as if it were yesterday—Carter holding out his hands and saying, "Pick up! Pick up!" over and over to him. Jonathan had frozen. His mother had always warned him to stay away from the Washingtons, and now, there he was, with one of them asking to be picked up.

"Pick up," Carter repeated, still holding out his hands.

Pointing at himself, Jonathan asked, "You talking to me?" He shot a glance back at his house to see if his mother was looking out the window. He wasn't even supposed to be on this side of the street, but he'd wanted to pass the slow-moving grandma out for her afternoon walk on the "right" sidewalk as he made his way home from school.

Carter hugged Jonathan's leg and smiled up at him.

Jonathan couldn't help himself—he bent down and picked up the little boy. "Hi, there." His eyes locked on the gaze of his young half brother.

Before he could do any further bonding, the little boy's mother rushed outside, grabbed her son out of Jonathan's grasp, and pulled him inside the house.

The Carter Washington who stepped forward was unmistakably the same one he'd met all those years ago. As he handed him his award, Jonathan's heart thudded as he met the gaze of the man who had accompanied the young man on stage. He was staring directly into the eyes of Philip Washington, the man who'd had a hand in his birth, the man who sent child support checks but had never wanted anything to do with him.

"Thank you, sir," Carter was saying. "I've improved my grades, so I'll graduate with honors, and I'm gonna make something of

225

myself, just like you did. I promise. I've already been accepted at UNC–Chapel Hill—your alma mater."

Jonathan wanted to say something encouraging—something that would motivate the young man to hit the books and leave the partying to the other kids. But he couldn't get his mouth to open.

"Cat got your tongue?" Philip sneered. "You can't even say hello to your little brother?" He snatched the certificate from Carter's grasp and flung it in Jonathan's face. "You've already insulted your brother by awarding him a lousy year of paid tuition, while those snot-nosed brats down over there get to enjoy a free ride for four years." He tossed his head at the previous groups as he dropped the certificate on the floor and stepped on it. "Keep it. We don't need your charity." He grabbed hold of Carter's arm. "Come on, Son. We'll find another way to get you through college."

The room fell silent; nothing was heard but the sound of Philip's boots as he stomped across the stage with Carter scurrying behind. As he passed Jonathan, Carter whispered, "Thank you."

Not knowing what else to do, Jonathan called up the last recipient and handed off her award. Then he turned off the podium mic, stepped off the stage, and left through the back door of the banquet hall.

Order your copy and finish reading this story today!

About the Author

Vanessa Miller is a best-selling author, entrepreneur, playwright, and motivational speaker. She started writing as a child, spending countless hours either reading or writing poetry, short stories, stage plays and novels. Vanessa's creative endeavors took on new meaning in1994 when she became a Christian. Since then, her writing has been centered on themes of redemption, often focusing on characters facing multi-dimensional struggles.

Vanessa's novels have received rave reviews, with several appearing on *Essence Magazine's* Bestseller's List. Miller's work has receiving numerous awards, including "Best Christian Fiction Mahogany Award" and the "Red Rose Award for Excellence in Christian Fiction." Miller graduated from Capital University with a degree in Organizational Communication. She is an ordained minister in her church, explaining, "God has called me to minister to readers and to help them rediscover their place with the Lord."

She has worked with numerous publishers: Urban Christian, Kimani Romance, Abingdon Press and Whitaker House. She is currently working on the Let's Stay Together series.

In 2016, Vanessa launched the Christian Book Lover's Retreat in an effort to bring readers and authors of Christian fiction together in an environment that's all about Faith, Fun & Fellowship. To learn more about Vanessa, please visit her website: www.vanessamiller.com. If you would like to know more about the Christian Book Lover's

Retreat that is currently held in Charlotte, NC during the last week in October you can visit:

http://www.christianbookloversretreat.com/index.html

Don't forget to join my mailing list:
http://vanessamiller.com/events/join-mailing-list/
Join me on Facebook: https://www.facebook.com/groups/
77899021863/
Join me on Twitter: https://www.twitter.com/vanessamiller01

CPSIA information can be obtained
at www.ICGtesting.com
Printed in the USA
LVHW080609251121
704427LV00010B/867